What a wedding night!

Zach had promised Susan their marriage would be on her terms, but he hadn't realized how difficult that promise was going to be to keep. Susan was a beautiful woman. But when she had confessed she'd never been in a hotel room before, he'd wanted to cuddle her against him and tell her he'd make her first experience one to remember.

He wanted to share a first with her.

What had started out as a simple scheme to please Gramp had become quite complicated.

Zach groaned and set up his bed on the couch.

It was going to be a long, lonely wedding night.

* * * *

And don't miss the other Lucky Charms!
Kate: Marry Me, Kate (SR #1344)
Maggie: Baby in Her Arms (SR #1350)

Dear Reader,

March roars in like a lion at Silhouette Romance, starting with popular author Susan Meier and *Husband from 9 to 5,* her exciting contribution to LOVING THE BOSS, a six-book series in which office romance leads to happily-ever-after. In this sparkling story, a bump on the head has a boss-loving woman believing she's married to the man of her dreams....

In March 1998, beloved author Diana Palmer launched VIRGIN BRIDES. This month, *Callaghan's Bride* not only marks the anniversary of this special Romance promotion, but it continues her wildly successful LONG, TALL TEXANS series! As a rule, hard-edged, hard-bodied Callaghan Hart distrusted sweet, virginal, starry-eyed young ladies. But ranch cook Tess Brady had this cowboy hankerin' to break all his rules.

Judy Christenberry's LUCKY CHARM SISTERS miniseries resumes with a warm, emotional pretend engagement story that might just lead to *A Ring for Cinderella.* When a jaded attorney delivers a very pregnant stranger's baby, he starts a journey toward healing...and making this woman his *Texas Bride,* the heartwarming new novel by Kate Thomas. In *Soldier and the Society Girl* by Vivian Leiber, the month's HE'S MY HERO selection, sparks fly when a true-blue, true-grit American hero requires the protocol services of a refined blue blood. A lone-wolf lawman meets his match in an indomitable schoolteacher—and her moonshining granny—in Gayle Kaye's *Sheriff Takes a Bride,* part of FAMILY MATTERS.

Enjoy this month's fantastic offerings, and make sure to return each and every month to Silhouette Romance!

Mary-Theresa Hussey

Mary-Theresa Hussey
Senior Editor, Silhouette Romance

Please address questions and book requests to:
Silhouette Reader Service
U.S.: 3010 Walden Ave., P.O. Box 1325, Buffalo, NY 14269
Canadian: P.O. Box 609, Fort Erie, Ont. L2A 5X3

JUDY CHRISTENBERRY

A RING FOR CINDERELLA

Silhouette

ROMANCE™

Published by Silhouette Books

America's Publisher of Contemporary Romance

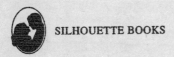

SILHOUETTE BOOKS

ISBN 0-373-19356-4

A RING FOR CINDERELLA

Copyright © 1999 by Judy Christenberry

Printed in U.S.A.

Books by Judy Christenberry

Silhouette Romance

The Nine-Month Bride #1324
*Marry Me, Kate #1343
*Baby in Her Arms #1350
*A Ring for Cinderella #1356

* Lucky Charm Sisters

JUDY CHRISTENBERRY

has been writing romances for fifteen years because she loves happy endings as much as her readers do. She's a bestselling author for Harlequin American Romance, but she has a long love of traditional romances and is delighted to tell a story that brings those elements to the reader. Judy quit teaching French recently and devotes her time to writing. She hopes readers have as much fun reading her stories as she does writing them. She spends her spare time reading, watching her favorite sports teams and keeping track of her two daughters. Judy's a native Texan, living in Plano, a suburb of Dallas.

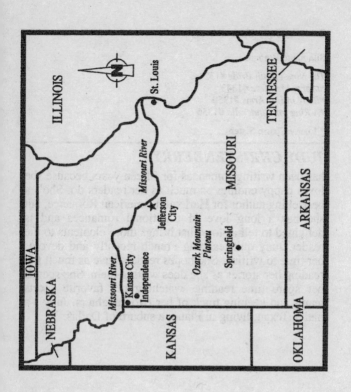

Chapter One

"More coffee?"

Without lifting his head, Zach Lowery moved his lips in a sham of a smile and nudged his cup toward the end of the table. He stared at the hand holding the glass pot. It was not the hand of the waitress who'd been serving him breakfast, which had been rather red and slightly wrinkled.

This hand was creamy smooth with rose polish adorning its trim nails. His gaze traveled up her arm and reached a face even more beautiful than his ex-wife's. Soft blond curls framed a delicate face, blue eyes, dark lashes and soft pink cheeks that were growing rosier as he stared.

"Can I get you anything else?" she asked in a husky voice that sizzled through his veins.

Yeah, she could. She could get him some peace for his grandfather, some redemption for himself. All he had to do was find out who she was and get her to play along with his plan.

"Who are you?" he demanded, his voice sounding like he hadn't used it in years.

She looked startled. Then, seeming to compose herself, she gave a half smile and said, "Susan."

He let his gaze roam over her. She had a knockout body, wrapped in soft blue knit, the kind of body men dreamed of.

Gramp would believe him if he brought Susan along.

"Susan, you want to get engaged?"

Susan Greenwood was tired. Tired of the money problems that had been her mother's legacy. Tired of being a single parent to her younger half siblings, Paul and Megan. Tired of putting up a brave front with her older half sisters, Kate and Maggie.

Since her older half sisters had discovered her existence a little over a year ago, the pair had offered her assistance with her problems. As much as she'd come to love Kate and Maggie, she was too proud to shift her burdens to their shoulders. They said she was too hardheaded.

And she was tired of men thinking she was hot to trot because she had a well-endowed figure and blond hair.

But she wasn't going to be rude to a customer at the Lucky Charm Diner, even if he had just proposed to her. She wouldn't do that to Kate.

"No, thanks." She even added a smile as she turned away.

"Wait!"

"You need something else?" She kept her words and her gaze cool, daring him to come on to her again.

"I didn't mean that the way it sounded." He ran a large hand through his dark hair. "Look, I can explain."

"Not necessary. Enjoy your meal." Again she turned away and reached the safety of the counter. "You'll have to serve that guy next time," she told Brenda, the waitress. "He wants to marry me."

"I should have such luck!" the middle-aged waitress exclaimed. "'Course, Jerry might object if I threw him over for some cowboy, even if he is handsome."

Susan smiled and went through the swinging door, past the kitchen to the small office behind it. She helped Brenda when there was a rush at the diner, or when Susan wanted a cup of coffee herself, but her real job was public relations.

She settled into her office chair with a sigh. She'd just started this job a week ago. It certainly beat her old job. She'd received propositions there, too, but they hadn't involved marriage. She gave a rueful smile and picked up the brochure she was designing.

Maybe she should ask that cowboy to pose for the front cover. They'd get a lot of female customers for the catering business if he did. With a sigh, she tried to dismiss his broad shoulders and hazel eyes. A man wasn't part of her plans, business or otherwise.

"Susan?" Brenda called as she pushed open the door. "That cowboy's insisting he talk to you. And I've got my hands full with customers. Want me to call the police?"

Susan needed to avoid such a scene if she could. It wouldn't do the diner's reputation any good to be associated with a police incident. "I'll see if I can talk him into leaving."

When she reached the counter where the cowboy, his Stetson on his head, was waiting, she noted his stern features, his square jaw. He wasn't going to be easy to dismiss.

"Yes?"

"Susan, I need to talk to you."

"We serve good food, but conversation isn't on the menu." She tried to keep her expression pleasant, but the steeliness of his stare made her uneasy.

"I'm not looking for conversation. I have a proposition for you."

"Yes, I've already heard it, and my answer is no." She turned around to return to her office, but he reached out and caught her arm before she could get away.

His hard, calloused hand held her firmly but not tightly. "All I'm asking you to do is listen to what I have to say. Give me ten minutes, in that booth," he said, gesturing to the last booth in the back, the one he'd earlier occupied. "If the answer is still no, I'll leave and not bother you anymore."

Susan debated her options. She could refuse and call the police. But she'd rather not. Maybe she could listen, then say no, and hope he kept his word. If not, then they'd definitely have a disturbance on their hands.

"Okay. Would you like more coffee while we talk?"

He stared at her. "You're not going to run away?"

"No." She was glad she was used to hiding her feelings. She didn't want this cowboy to know she was trembling inside.

He released her arm, drawing his hand back slowly, and nodded. She picked up the coffeepot and two clean cups and saucers. Then she walked the length of the counter, slipped through the opening and continued on to the back booth.

He was right behind her. When he slid into the booth, their knees knocked together and she jumped in surprise.

"Sorry. I've got long legs," he said.

She'd realized that. The man was easily over six foot. She filled the cups of coffee, saying nothing. But she did check the time on her watch.

"I've got ten minutes," he reminded her, his jaw clenched.

She nodded.

Zach couldn't figure out how to start. Finally, he blurted out, "My grandfather is dying."

He'd shocked her, but he didn't know how else to explain his sudden proposal. "He's been wanting me to marry, have babies.'' He stopped and stared out the windows, ashamed of what he had to confess. ''I lied to him. I told him I had a woman...a fiancée. He seemed pleased.''

He stopped to take a sip of coffee, but he avoided looking at the beautiful woman across from him. ''Then today he had a massive heart attack.'' He paused again, this time to swallow the emotion that filled him.

''I'm sorry,'' she said softly, in that husky voice.

His gaze hardened. He'd been misled before by a beautiful face and a sweet voice. Women used their softness to trap a man.

''He wants to meet my fiancée.''

He watched her carefully as comprehension filled her gaze. ''I see. And you want me to—''

''Pretend to be my fiancée.''

''I appreciate your predicament, but—''

''I'll pay you!'' He was desperate. She was a beautiful woman, the kind Gramp would expect him to choose. And he didn't have much time.

''No, I—''

''Ten thousand dollars.''

He watched cynically as the amount he'd offered penetrated her brain. Then he leaned back against the cushioned bench. ''Not bad for one night's work, is it?''

She stared at him. ''Define 'night.'''

He gave her a look of disgust. ''Lady, I don't have to pay for that kind of evening. I'm talking about a visit to the intensive care unit at the hospital. It won't take long. He—he doesn't have a lot of strength.''

"You're serious?"

Suddenly, weariness hit him. What had he been hoping? That this woman, in spite of her incredible beauty, would put someone else's needs before her own? *Yeah, right.*

"Can you afford to—"

He whipped out his checkbook. "Ever heard of the Lowery Ranch?"

She nodded, frowning.

"Well, I'm the heir to the Lowery Ranch. I can afford it." He scrawled his name on the check and ripped it out of his checkbook. "Here's five thousand now. You've got time to put it in the bank before it closes. I'll give you the other five thousand when it's over."

She stared at the check as if she couldn't believe it. Then she slowly reached out and picked it up from the table.

"What's your last name and address?"

She answered him as if in a daze, and he jotted down the information. She didn't live in the best part of town, he realized.

"I'll pick you up at six-thirty. Be ready."

Then he walked out of the diner.

Susan continued to stare at the check for long minutes after the stranger's departure. Five thousand dollars. She couldn't believe it.

Her half sister's room and board at college was due

in two weeks. Megan would be a freshman and had gotten a scholarship for her tuition. All she needed was living expenses to go as long as Susan could come up with the money. And suddenly, here it was.

She knew she should tear the check up. In fact, she'd been considering offering to help the man, but there was her eight-year-old brother, Paul, to consider. Before she could decide, the cowboy had thrown his money in her face.

If he truly was the Lowery heir, he had plenty to spare. And she was going to do him a service, pretending to be his fiancée. But all the justification in the world didn't ease her conscience.

Deliberately, she folded the check. Her conscience would have to live with it. She wasn't going to turn down the opportunity to pay for Megan's living expenses at college, maybe even finish paying off her mother's debts, buy Paul a few clothes for when he started school. She couldn't afford to let this opportunity go.

She'd been parent and sister to both of her younger half siblings for four years now. Her mother had died when Susan was twenty-one. She'd just finished her junior year in school, existing on a scholarship and a part-time job as a waitress.

Suddenly, she had to provide for Megan and Paul, as well as herself. And deal with her mother's debts. All her plans, her dreams, had disappeared as she faced her responsibilities.

She'd had a surprise eighteen months ago when she acquired two more half sisters and learned of her father, and that he'd just died. Her new sisters assured her her father had only found out about her existence just before his death. Her mother, when she'd asked questions as a child, had told her her father had moved on. He hadn't been interested in her.

Neither had the other men her mother had been with. Each time the men disappeared, her mother was left with a child and no support. Susan had grown up ashamed of her mother and her behavior. When Paul's and Megan's fathers had disappeared also, Susan had felt responsible for helping to raise her half siblings.

Kate and Maggie, her new half sisters, were wonderful, and the feeling of not being alone anymore made a huge difference to Susan. Even financially, she'd gained. The diner, where she now worked, had been her father's. She was actually part-owner, with Kate and Maggie, though she'd protested their including her.

And when, last week, she'd quit her public relations job with a local firm because her boss wouldn't leave her alone, Kate had immediately hired her for the Lucky Charm Diner and Catering Company. But they were just beginning to show a profit, and the salary was less than she'd been making.

She couldn't turn down the money the cowboy had offered her.

As weird as his offer was, at least she would be earning the money and not taking charity from her new family.

She slid out of the booth. "Brenda, I'm going to leave a few minutes early today."

The waitress only nodded.

She'd been careful to adhere to a strict work schedule in the week she'd been there. She didn't want anyone to think she'd taken advantage of Kate. But this was an exception. It was four-thirty. She could get to the drive-through window of the bank before it closed, just as the cowboy had said.

What if he wasn't who he said he was? What if the check bounced higher than a skyscraper? She sighed as she picked up her purse from beside her desk. She'd find out soon enough, and if it wasn't any good, she'd be no worse off than she was now.

Which was flat broke.

After depositing the check, she hurried home. Paul spent his days with her neighbor. Rosa Cavalho had an eight-year-old, too, Manuel, and he and Paul were best friends. What Susan paid Rosa helped their tight budget, and it ensured that Paul was safe.

In two more weeks, school would start. Then her baby-sitting fees would go down. But Paul's appetite seemed to increase each year. Her grocery bill was growing along with him.

"Rosa?" she called as she rapped on the apartment door across from hers.

It swung open, and two little boys looked at her in surprise. "You're early!" Paul exclaimed. Then he gave her a big smile and hugged her waist. "Hi!"

"Hi, yourself. How's everything?"

"Who is it?" Rosa called. She did sewing at home to add to her husband's construction income.

"It's me," Susan called as she headed to Rosa's bedroom, where she worked. "Could you keep Paul this evening for a couple of hours?"

"Oh, Susan, I'm sorry, but we have to go to my mother-in-law's tonight. It's a command performance," Rosa said with sarcasm. Her husband's family didn't like Rosa because she was from a poor family and hadn't increased her husband's financial worth.

"That's okay. I'll just have to take Paul with me."

"You have a date?" Rosa asked, hope in her voice. She worried that Susan didn't get out much.

"No, it's sort of a job, but Paul won't get in the way. He can sit in the lounge. What's the occasion at your mother-in-law's?"

Rosa made a face. "Pedro's sister is in town with her wealthy husband."

"Looks like we'll both have an exciting evening," Susan said with a laugh. "I'll take Paul home now."

In spite of Paul's protests, Susan insisted he come with her. Those protests were nothing compared to the ones he made when he discovered he had to bathe and put on his one pair of nice slacks and a clean shirt.

"I can stay by myself, Susan. I'm eight now. I don't need to go with you."

She smiled down at his earnest expression. "Sweetie, I know you're eight. But I can't leave you alone at night. Besides, it will be interesting. You haven't been to a hospital since you were born.''

Scowling, he dragged his feet to the door of his room. ''I won't have a good time.''

''Sometimes, we don't. But we do what we have to, right?'' It was a lesson she'd learned long ago.

''Yeah,'' he agreed, resignation in his voice.

''Go ahead and take your shower now, Paul, while I figure out what we're going to eat for dinner. I'll need the bathroom after we eat.''

Some day they were going to have more than one bathroom. When Megan was home, she and her sister had to share the larger bedroom, leaving Paul the smaller room for himself. Her dream was to have a home where everyone had his or her own space.

Megan had gone to the University of Nebraska early for orientation and to find a job. Although like Susan, Megan had gotten a scholarship for her tuition, she still intended to help Susan pay for her room and board.

Which brought Susan's thoughts back to this evening. As she opened a can of tuna to add to the casserole she was making, she justified her behavior in taking the money again.

They were good reasons.

And had nothing to do with the handsomeness of the cowboy. But she couldn't deny his good looks affected her. Not that anything would come of it, of course. But he was a sexy man.

And for an hour, she would be his fiancée.

* * *

Zach went to his favorite store on the Plaza and bought everything he'd need to dress for the evening. Then he checked into a nearby hotel.

It was difficult to think of practical matters after what the doctors had told him about his grandfather. The one person he loved more than anyone else on earth could die at any moment. His grandfather had had a heart attack this morning. They'd flown him by helicopter to Kansas City and finally stabilized him, but it had been touch-and-go.

Dear God, he loved that old man.

And why wouldn't he? Gramp had been there for him all his life, had become his only parent when his mom and dad had died in a car accident when he was eight.

Gramp had given him hugs as well as a whack on his rear when he'd needed them. He'd taught Zach ranching and manners.

He'd taught him to be a man.

And Zach had failed him.

The one thing Gramp had wanted was for Zach to marry. To provide sons to carry on the ranch traditions that had gone on for four generations. He'd tried. Five years ago, he'd married a beautiful woman, sure he'd found his own true love.

He snorted in disgust. That marriage hadn't worked out. No marriage. No heirs.

Which brought him back to Susan Greenwood.

An hour later, he settled into the dining room of the hotel and ordered a steak with all the trimmings. He'd talked to the doctor before he'd come down to dinner and Gramp was holding his own, looking forward to Zach's arrival that evening with his fiancée.

Gramp was like a dog with one bone. He never left it alone. He wanted great-grandsons.

Too bad making babies wasn't part of the deal with Susan, he decided with a wry smile. The lady was one tasty morsel. But he'd had enough of women with cash-register hearts. He might enjoy a night spent with one every once in a while. Hell, he was a man. But he wasn't about to give any of them legal or emotional control over him or anything that belonged to him.

But Gramp's happiness was important to him.

That was why he was dressed in a sport coat, slacks, crisp white shirt and, worst of all, a tie. He hated those things. But tonight was important. If he'd come to the hospital in his jeans to introduce his fiancée, Gramp would be offended.

After paying his bill, he settled his Stetson on his head and headed for the rental car. Since he'd traveled on the helicopter with Gramp to Kansas City, he didn't have his pickup with him. Instead, he had to fit his big frame into a four-door sedan.

He'd gotten directions from the concierge before leaving the hotel, just to be sure he had the right area of town. As he drove, the neighborhoods changed from the elegant to the barely habitable.

Pulling up in front of an apartment building with peeling paint and a small patch of grass that hadn't been mowed any too recently, he frowned. Had he made a mistake? Susan had looked high-class, though he now realized she'd worn no jewelry other than plain gold earrings.

He got out of the car and locked the door. Checking the address once more, he headed for the stairs in the center of the building. When he found the apartment on the second floor, he rapped firmly.

The door swung open, and he had to drop his gaze to look at the person who had opened the door. A little boy stared up at him.

"Hello. I'm looking for Susan Greenwood."

"Okay. Susan?" the boy called. "He's here." Then he turned back around to stare up at Zach. "I'm ready."

That gave Zach pause. "Uh, okay. Where are you going?"

"With you. But I don't want to."

Chapter Two

"Paul, that was ill-mannered. Apologize to Mr. Lowery, please," Susan called as she entered the living room of their apartment.

Then she looked at Zach Lowery.

Gone was the scruffy outdoorsman in his tight jeans and Western shirt. In his place was a clean-shaven, expensively dressed man. Handsome as sin.

She also realized she recognized him. His picture was in the society pages frequently. But he was usually dressed in a tux with a beautiful woman on his arm.

All that remained of the cowboy she'd met earlier today was his hat.

"I'm sorry about Paul, but I couldn't get a sitter. And I promise he'll be well behaved." She lifted her chin as she met his glare. Her arm stole around Paul's thin shoulders, afraid the man would hurt her brother's feelings.

Zach Lowery looked down at Paul, and Susan was relieved to see his glare soften. "I'm sure he will be. Are you ready?"

"Yes," she agreed, releasing a sigh of relief. She picked up her purse. As Paul preceded her, she pulled the door closed behind her, making sure it was locked.

"How long have you lived here?" Zach asked as they went down the stairs.

She frowned. Why would he want to know that? She didn't expect friendship from the man. In fact, she'd decided to keep anything personal out of their agreement. Then she wouldn't feel quite so bad about taking his money.

"About four years," she finally said when she couldn't think of a reason not to answer. This place had been all they could afford after her mother's death, but she definitely wasn't going to tell him that.

"It's not a very safe neighborhood."

"I thought you didn't live in Kansas City," she said, not about to have an out-of-towner criticize her home.

"We're only about fifty miles out of town. I do come to Kansas City occasionally," he assured her dryly.

"Yes, I've seen you in the society pages."

He ignored her words and led the way to a shiny blue car.

"Wow," Paul said with a sigh. "I like your car."

Susan hurriedly hid her smile. Considering the wreck she drove, Paul's enthusiasm was understandable. Zach Lowery probably couldn't understand his reaction.

"It's a rental, but thanks," he said, smiling at her brother.

Maybe he was a nice man, after all. She hadn't been sure after he had left the diner.

He came to the passenger side of the car and opened the door. Such attention flustered her. She wasn't used to it. "Oh, I have to make sure Paul gets his seat belt on," she said, not slipping into the seat as he expected.

"I can fasten my own seat belt," Paul protested. He was definitely well past the helpless stage.

"Of course you can. And I'll show you how these work. They're a little tricky," the man said with a kind smile. He waited until Susan had gotten seated, closed her door, then opened the door for Paul. Susan turned and watched over her shoulder as the two males conferred over the seat belt.

Once they were under way, she cleared her throat. After doing some thinking about the evening in front of her, she'd concluded she and her co-conspirator needed to get their stories straight. "I think we need to talk."

"Want more money?" he asked in a low voice that she hoped Paul couldn't hear.

"No! I meant we should match our stories. I don't know anything about you. Or you me."

"I'm thirty-three, been married once and divorced

after three miserable years. No children. I live at the ranch. I attended Kansas University. I like sports, country-western music and beautiful women.'' He clicked off his preferences in a rapid-fire fashion, leaving Susan stunned.

When she said nothing, trying to sort out the information he'd given her, he said, ''Well? Aren't you going to tell me about yourself?''

''Of course, I—I'm twenty-five. I work for the Lucky Charm Diner and Catering Company. I'm doing public relations and—and the advertising campaign. I graduated from the University of Missouri here in Kansas City.''

He pulled the car into the hospital parking lot. ''And you have Paul.''

Susan realized he was under the misapprehension that Paul was her son, but what did it matter? Paul was hers, whether she'd given birth to him or not. And it eliminated the need to reveal her mother's sordid past. That information was definitely personal.

''Grampy won't have the strength to ask much,'' he continued. ''I'll do all the talking. If I don't know the answer, I'll make one up. After all, he…it won't matter what I say.''

The emotion in his voice was the sexiest thing about Zach Lowery, and that was saying a lot. He was a man who cared about his grandfather to the point of doing *anything* to ensure his happiness.

She nodded.

''Is your grandfather sick?'' Paul asked from the back seat.

She started to hush her brother, but Zach answered first.

"Yeah, buddy, he is."

"Are the doctors going to make him better?"

This time Susan spoke first. "Paul, you mustn't ask questions right now. And be very quiet in the hospital. Some people will be trying to sleep."

He liked the kid.

And Susan was right. He was well behaved.

Zach led the way down the long corridor to the intensive care unit. Susan followed, holding Paul's hand. "Is there a lounge where Paul can wait?" she whispered, surprising him.

"He can go in with us. They won't stop us. Gramp knows the right people." When they reached the door, Zach signaled to one of the nurses.

"The doctor said we could see my grandfather," he said softly, sure the doctor had left word with the nurse. He didn't want any battles tonight. But there would be one if they tried to interfere.

"Yes, Mr. Lowery. The doctor warned us. Come this way."

She led them into a bare room, the only furniture a large bed in the center. His grandfather looked so small, lying there with tubes in him. He'd always been a big man, strong and active.

"Gramp?" Zach said softly as he moved to the head of the bed, touching his grandfather's shoulder.

The old man came awake slowly. "Huh? That you, boy?" he asked groggily.

Zach fought to keep tears from his eyes. "Yeah, it's me, Gramp. I kept my promise. I brought Susan to see you." He motioned for Susan to join him, watching his grandfather as she stepped forward. The sudden spark in the old man's eyes told Zach he'd done the right thing.

"Hello, Mr. Lowery," Susan said softly, her voice husky and sweet. Without any prompting, she reached out and clasped his wrinkled hand. "I'm pleased to meet you."

"Me, too, girl. Me, too." He struggled to sit up, and Susan quickly helped him arrange another pillow beneath his head.

"Would you like me to raise the bed a little?"

"Yeah, that'd be good." He leaned back in relief.

Zach watched as Susan helped his grandfather get comfortable. He was getting his money's worth, he'd have to say that.

"Who's that?" Pete Lowery demanded, staring at Paul, who'd followed Susan around the end of the bed.

Zach had forgotten about the boy.

Susan spoke before he could think what to say. "Paul's mine. I think he's the reason Zach hadn't said much about me. He wasn't sure how you'd feel about a ready-made family."

Zach stared at her, stunned by her words. Her explanation made sense, but he hadn't planned out that much in advance.

"Shame on you, Zach. You know I love kids. Come here, boy. What's your name?"

Susan eased Paul forward, holding his shoulders as he stood next to the bed.

"Paul," the little boy whispered.

"You'd be about what, seven, eight years old?"

"Eight."

"Your ma must've been a baby when you were born," Pete teased.

Paul didn't know how to answer, turning to look at Susan.

"Yeah, she was," Zach answered, deciding it was time he took over the conversation. "Has the doctor been in to see you? How did he say you were doing?"

Pete waved away Zach's questions. "Don't want to talk about that stuff. Susan, tell me, has this scalawag been good to you?"

She smiled. "Very good."

As well she should say, Zach thought cynically. She was being well paid. But he had to admit she was giving great value. Gramp liked her, he could tell.

"So why haven't—" Pete broke off and grimaced, drawing Zach's attention.

"You shouldn't talk so much," he urged, stepping closer and touching his grandfather's shoulder. Susan stepped forward and tucked in the cover that had come loose.

"Nonsense. It was just a twinge," Pete insisted. "I want to know when you two are going to get hitched."

"What's 'hitched' mean?" Paul asked, looking puzzled.

"Married, boy, married. Don't you want a new daddy?" Pete asked, his gaze on Paul's face.

Zach almost swallowed his tongue. "Uh, Gramp, that's not, I mean, we haven't set a date."

"Why not? You're not getting any younger. Me, neither." He sighed, sort of fading into the pillows, which only underlined to Zach how little time he had left with his grandfather.

"That's not important right now. We want to concentrate all our attention on getting you well."

"You want to get me well? Then get yourself married to this little lady. Now, before it's too late for me to see you happy." His breathing was becoming noisier and his eyes were closing.

"I think your grandfather is tiring himself out," Susan said, her soft hands pulling the covers higher again before she tenderly cupped Pete's cheek. "You need to rest, Mr. Lowery. Paul and I will go to the waiting room and give you a little time alone with Zach."

Pete's eyes came open again. "You're a sweetheart, Susan. You take good care of my boy, okay?"

She leaned down and kissed his cheek. "You just take care of yourself. Zach's a big boy. He'll be all right."

Pete chuckled, a sound Zach hadn't been sure he'd ever hear again. "Yep, you're a sweetheart."

Zach's gaze met Susan's as she and Paul walked past him. On a sudden urge, he caught her arm and bent down to brush her lips with his.

He only did it to persuade Gramp everything was

on the up-and-up. And to thank Susan for a great performance. His action had nothing to do with the fact that he hadn't been able to get her off his mind all afternoon. Or those luscious lips of hers.

Nope, nothing to do with those things.

Thankfully she wasn't facing Gramp, because she appeared startled by his action.

"I'll be out in a few minutes," he assured her, and winked at Paul.

They slipped from the room.

"Now, tell me why you haven't married her," Gramp ordered, his voice sounding much stronger all of a sudden.

"Why did that man kiss you?" Paul asked as soon as they were in the waiting room.

"Because—because he—I don't know." Susan knew, but she didn't want to explain to Paul that she and Zach were lying to Zach's grandfather.

"I like him."

She looked at her little brother in surprise. The few times she'd accepted a date, Paul had been...difficult. "Zach?"

"Yeah. And his grandfather, too. Why don't I have a grandfather?"

It wasn't the first time Paul had questioned her about his family. She gave her standard answer. "You had two grandfathers, just like everyone else, sweetie, but they died before you were born."

"Oh."

"Look, here's a television. Want me to turn it on? I think Monday night football is playing."

"Okay."

Paul wasn't very enthusiastic, because he intended to be a baseball player, but football was better than nothing.

And maybe it would keep him from asking more uncomfortable questions.

Half an hour later, Zach came into the room.

"How is he?" she asked, surprised at how much she cared about the old man's health. After all, she didn't really know him.

"Better. The doctor's with him now." He paced around the room, impatient, ignoring both her and Paul.

"Your grandfather is a nice man," Paul said softly, his gaze following Zach's movement rather than the football game.

Susan feared Zach might be irritated by Paul's comment, because it interrupted his private battles. Instead, the man walked over to Paul and touched his shoulder. "Yeah. He is, isn't he?" Then he sat down by Paul.

"What's the score?"

The little boy supplied the information, and the two bonded in typical male fashion.

Then the doctor came into the room.

Zach bounded up from the couch and met the doctor before he'd made much progress into the room. Susan couldn't hear their conversation, but she watched them all the same.

Finally the doctor left the room.

"I'm going to say good-night to Gramp. I'll be back in a minute," Zach murmured.

"Then we'll go home?" Paul asked, yawning. "I'm sleepy."

"Then we'll go home, sweetie," Susan responded as Zach left the room. "Thanks for being so good."

"It's okay. I'm going to pretend Gramp is my grandfather. Is that okay, Susan? I won't tell him, but since I don't have a grandfather, I'll just pretend."

Susan gave her brother a hug. "As long as you don't say anything to Zach or his grandfather, then that's okay."

Zach returned. "Ready to go?"

Susan studied his grim face as she helped Paul off the sofa. Something was wrong. She feared the doctor's news hadn't been good. "Do you want us to take a taxi home, so you can stay here?"

"No. They have my number and will call if there's any change." His words were abrupt, clipped, as if he were out of patience.

She made no more suggestions.

Once they were in the car, heading back to her apartment, she asked, "Are you going back to the ranch tonight?"

"No, I'm staying in town."

He didn't volunteer where, and she didn't ask. If she'd had more room, she would've offered to let him stay with them, but somehow she couldn't see Zach Lowery stretched out on their lumpy couch.

There were several men hanging around outside the

apartment building when they pulled up, and Zach scowled in their direction. "This isn't a safe neighborhood."

Susan, recognizing Manuel's father, smiled and waved before turning to Zach. "We're perfectly safe. Those are some of our neighbors."

Opening the car door, she slipped out of the car and reached for Paul's door. Before she could get the boy out, Zach was at her side.

"I'll walk you upstairs."

"Really, that's not necessary." She started to thank him for a lovely evening until she realized she'd been working, not socializing.

"Yes, it is. I need to pay you."

He sounded angry. Fine, she didn't have to take the rest of the money. The first check would help her out of some financial difficulty. She opened her mouth to tell him, but he grabbed Paul's hand and her arm and started them toward the stairs at a fast clip.

"You're going too fast," Paul protested.

Without a word, Zach swung the boy up into his arms, then reattached himself to Susan's arm.

"Wow, you're strong," Paul said in awe.

For the first time since Zach Lowery had come into her life, he smiled, and Susan realized *handsome* didn't begin to describe him.

"You weigh a lot less than a bale of hay, Paul," he said to her brother. "You need to eat more."

"Susan says I eat lots and lots," the boy said with a giggle.

"Why do you call her Susan?" Zach asked, frowning.

"'Cause that's her name," Paul said simply.

Susan could've explained then that Paul was her brother, not her son, but the stairway didn't seem like a good place for such a private conversation. And she needed to keep her distance from such a handsome man—not get closer.

She got out her keys to open the door, relieved when Zach let go of her arm. His touch had bothered her. As the door swung open, she turned. "Thank you for seeing us to our door. I hope your grandfather's condition improves."

She pulled Paul in front of her and turned to go in, but she discovered Zach wasn't ready to leave. He followed her in.

"We need to talk."

"About what?"

"Payment, for one thing. Aren't you interested in the rest of your money?" He gave her a sardonic stare.

Her cheeks flushed as she ducked her head. "I think your first check was sufficient. I didn't do that much tonight."

"You more than fulfilled your end of the bargain. Put the boy to bed. Then we'll talk."

She didn't like him giving orders. But he was right. It was past Paul's bedtime, and the boy's eyelids were drooping. "Come on, Paul, let's get you tucked in. And you can read for a little while."

He was about to protest until she'd tacked on the

reward of reading. Paul loved books. "Can I read all of *Peter Pan?*"

That was his longest book and would prolong going to sleep for almost an hour. With a tender smile, she agreed. "Okay, but don't blame me if you don't want to get up in the morning."

"Do you have any *Hank, the Cow Dog* books?" Zach suddenly asked.

Paul halted on his way out of the room, a frown on his face. "No. Who's that?"

"I'll send you a couple. They're stories about a cow dog named Hank who takes care of a ranch."

"Wow!" Paul exclaimed, using his favorite word. "That'd be neat. When will you—"

"Paul," Susan intervened. "Say thank you."

"Thank you," he repeated, and flew across the room to hug Zach around the waist. "I can't wait."

Zach rubbed the boy's head. "I'll see that you get them right away."

With a bright smile on his face, Paul ran out of the room. Susan, after sending Zach an apologetic smile, followed him. Zach didn't realize what a treat new books were to Paul.

But she did. Gratitude filled her as she followed her brother.

What an appealing kid. He'd call a bookstore in the morning and have them send over whatever "Hank" books they had on hand.

As memory of what had occurred this evening came back, Zach began to pace the small room. What happened next depended a lot on Susan. And it could be costly to him. But he'd already invested ten thousand dollars in his grandfather's happiness. And it had paid off.

When he'd left tonight, Gramp was more relaxed than he'd been in quite a while. And he'd had a smile on his face.

Susan came back into the room.

"Is Paul in bed?"

"Yes. Thank you for offering to send him a book. He loves them."

"No problem."

There was an awkward moment as Zach tried to think of how to approach the difficult subject.

"Well," Susan said, a false brightness in her voice, "I won't keep you. I'm sure it's been a long day."

"Yes, it has, but we still have to talk." He reached in his coat pocket and pulled out his checkbook. Whether she agreed to his plan or not, she had earned the rest of her money for tonight.

"Oh, no! No more is necessary. I mean, the first check was very generous. And I didn't do much."

He stared at her, speculation in his eyes. In his experience, women didn't usually turn down money, whether they'd earned it or not. She must have some scheme already worked out in her head.

"You earned it."

"No, really. Your grandfather is a very nice man. I enjoyed meeting him."

"You brought him a lot of happiness." He wrote out the check and ripped it out. "Here."

"Zach, really, I don't feel right about taking the check."

"You'll change your mind when you hear what I'm going to ask you to do next."

Chapter Three

Susan stared at him, confused. "You mean you want me to visit your grandfather again?"

"Well, that's part of it," he said, not quite meeting her gaze.

"I'll be glad to visit him, but—"

"We have to get married."

He said those words calmly, in a normal tone of voice, as if what he said made sense.

She stared at him. "What did you say?"

"I said we have to get married."

She sank down onto the lumpy sofa, not sure her legs would hold her any longer. "That's—that's ridiculous."

"Yeah."

That was all, just that one laconic word, as if his bizarre statement didn't need any more comment. Slowly, she extended her hand, the one that held the check. "I think you'd better take this and go, Mr. Lowery."

"And break an old man's heart?" he asked softly, staring at her.

She immediately pictured Pete Lowery in his hospital bed, a sweet smile on his wrinkled face. "No! No, I don't want to...your grandfather...what are you talking about?"

"Gramp wants us to get married in his hospital room so he can be present. He said it's the only thing he'll ever ask of me. He begged me."

She didn't need to see the anguish in his eyes. It was in his voice. And she could feel it in her heart. "Oh, Zach, I'm sorry. That's terrible."

He crossed the room to sit down beside her. "I knew you'd understand. You were terrific tonight. You'll handle it well."

Suddenly things had gotten very personal. Exactly what she hadn't intended. "No! I mean, I didn't say I'd do it. You can't— It would be wrong to marry. No, I can't do it!" Just the thought of marrying Zach Lowery put her in a tizzy.

"How much?"

His cynical question, accompanied by a look that only underlined his opinion, brought sanity to Susan. "I don't want your money. And I don't want to lie to Mr. Lowery anymore. Go find someone else to play games with you."

He stood and paced across the room. "Good negotiating tactics, Susan. Refuse to do the job when you know you're the only one who can. He's already met you, believes you're my fiancée. I'm supposed to appear with another woman and convince him I've found a new fiancée in less than twenty-four hours?''

She bowed her head, trying to think through the situation she'd gotten herself into. "Okay. I realize you can't get anyone else. Can you talk your grandfather out of the marriage? Maybe we can—"

Anger filled his voice. "Sure I could. I'll just go tell him to forget it. I don't care if he dies happy. That'll do the trick."

She squared her jaw. He didn't have to be so...so difficult. "All right. Can we hire an actor to play the minister? Fake the marriage?"

"Gramp wants our minister from home to perform the ceremony."

"And you're willing to go ahead with this?"

"I have no choice. So, we're back to that question I asked earlier. How much? Because I can assure you, you won't be getting half my net worth, or my ranch from this...marriage. I'll be generous, but not that generous. Then when...when the pretense isn't necessary any longer, we'll part company."

Susan closed her eyes. The man was serious. "Did the doctor say how long?" She felt like a monster, asking that question, but she had to know.

"No," he responded, his voice a growl. "He said he couldn't make any predictions."

"So we get married, but nothing changes, right? It's a marriage in name only?"

He stepped closer. "It'll be whatever kind of marriage you want, honey. I wouldn't turn down a little...sharing, but whatever kind of marriage it is, it ends when Gramp—when it's not necessary anymore.''

She felt her cheeks flame as she considered his sardonic words. "Sharing" with this man would be devastating, or it would be when it ended. Somehow she knew that, probably because she shivered every time he touched her.

"No 'sharing.' We'll do what it takes for your grandfather to believe we're happily married, but that's all.'' She lifted her chin and stared him in the eyes. She wanted no misunderstandings.

"You still haven't answered my question. How much?''

She held up the check she still had in her hands. "This will do.''

"Come on, honey," he said, but his tone of voice didn't match the sweetness of his words, "you could get enough to move out of this dump."

"Please don't refer to my home in such a derogatory manner," she protested stiffly, straightening her spine.

He stared at her, disbelief in his eyes, but she didn't care. She refused to say anything else.

"Okay, fine," he snapped. "Tomorrow night. Gramp has the connections to speed things up. I'll pick you up at six-thirty again. Wear something bridal." Then he stomped out of her apartment, slamming the door behind him.

The next day, Susan stared at herself in the mirror. Something bridal. She only hoped the dress she'd chosen was what Zach Lowery had had in mind.

At first, she'd tried to find something in her limited wardrobe that she could wear. The closest she came was a blue wool suit. But since it was late August, she didn't think that would do.

Finally, she'd taken her lunch hour today and found an ivory dress, roaring twenties style, that Megan could use for parties at college. They were about the same size.

She'd added a wisp of a veil anchored to an ivory rose and ivory silk shoes.

And, most important of all, she'd kept quiet about her impending nuptials. She knew if she told Kate and Maggie, they'd insist she take their money, instead of earning it from Zach. And making his grandfather happy.

A rap on the door had her knees shaking. She drew a deep breath and, after checking the peephole, opened the door for Zach Lowery in a tux.

She didn't know how much more she could take.

He looked her up and down and smiled. "Nice."

"Thanks." She picked up her ivory bag and moved past him, waiting for him to move so she could lock the door.

"Where's Paul?"

"He's with a sitter."

"Gramp will expect him with us."

She'd thought about what she should do, but she felt it would be difficult for Paul to understand about the fake marriage. "I don't want to upset him."

"I don't, either. Either one of them. But Paul has to come. Gramp not only wouldn't understand why he wasn't there, but he also *wants* him there. He likes him."

"And Paul likes him. But how are you going to explain this situation to an eight-year-old?"

"We'll tell him the truth. We're getting married for a little while. For Gramp's sake." He stood there stern and unyielding, waiting for her to give in.

And she did. The situation was so bizarre, she couldn't decide what was right or wrong. With a sigh, she crossed the landing and knocked on Rosa's door.

When her friend answered, she told her Paul was going with her, instead of staying with them.

"Paul!" Rosa called over her shoulder. Then she turned back to Susan. "You look like a bride. Is there something you haven't told me?"

Susan barely smiled. "I'll have to explain later," she said as her brother appeared. "Paul, there's been a change in plans. You're coming with Zach and me. I need you to hurry up and change."

"Wow! You look neat, Susan," her brother said, staring at her.

"Thanks, sweetie. Go put on the slacks and shirt you wore last night. I hung them in your closet."

"But Manuel and me was gonna watch the baseball game," he said, frowning.

"Now, Paul," she said quietly but sternly.

His shoulders slumping, he crossed the hallway to their apartment.

"Hurry, please," she called after him. She said

good-night to Rosa and headed back to her own apartment in case Paul needed her.

Zach caught her arm as she moved past him. "Thank you for giving in on this. I want things to be perfect for Gramp."

"Yes, I know."

"I need you to sign this, too," he said, reaching inside his tux jacket as he followed her inside.

She frowned as he extended a paper to her. Taking it, she unfolded it and skimmed the contents. "I said you didn't have to pay me any more money!" The paper was an agreement stating that she would marry him for an additional ten thousand dollars. When the marriage ended, she would not be eligible for any more compensation.

"That's your only complaint?" he asked, one eyebrow rising.

"Why would I complain? I agreed to these terms last night without the extra money." And she found his assumption that she would want more insulting.

"Okay. Here's a pen."

She snatched it from his hand. Fine. She'd sign his silly agreement. And if he really did pay her an additional ten thousand dollars, she'd be able to pay Megan's room and board the second semester, too.

She handed him the signed paper with no comment, and they stood in silence until Paul reappeared.

"You forgot to change your shoes, buddy," Zach said as the little boy finished buttoning up his shirt.

Paul looked at Susan, a puzzled look on his face.

"Those are the only shoes Paul has," she said softly.

Her cheeks flushed as he stared her up and down, no doubt assessing the cost of her attire. She didn't try to explain that she'd used part of his money to look nice for the occasion.

"Sorry, Paul, you look fine. Ready to go? By the way, I've got those books I promised you in the car."

The boy's face lit up. "Wow! Really?"

"Really," Zach said with a smile.

He might be a jerk with her, but he was kind to Paul. Susan swallowed her anger.

"Why do I have to go?" Paul asked. "Susan said tonight was only for adults."

"Well, Susan was wrong. It's for adults and one special little boy. I'll explain all about it in the car."

Zach was making plans to take Paul on a shopping trip before he walked out of his life again. The woman beside him, looking pure and innocent in her bridal attire, probably would spend all the money he'd paid her on herself.

"When are you going to explain?" Paul asked, drawing his attention.

"Sorry, Paul, I forgot. My grandfather really wants me to get married. But I don't have time to find a real bride, so Susan is going to pretend to be my wife. To make Gramp happy. Can you keep our secret?"

"Sure. But why do I have to be there?"

"Well, if it were your mom's *real* wedding, you'd

be there, wouldn't you?'' He smiled in the rearview mirror.

''Yeah, I guess, if she was alive,'' Paul said with a sigh. ''All my family is dead 'cept Susan and Megan.''

Zach almost lost control of the steering wheel in his shock. Then he turned to stare at Susan. ''You're not his mother?''

''No, I'm his sister and legal guardian.'' She never even looked at him.

''Why didn't you say that last night?'' It galled him that she'd kept the truth from him.

''You didn't ask, and I didn't think it mattered.''

''Who is Megan?'' he snapped, too irritated to respond to her remark.

''She's our sister,'' Paul said from the back seat. ''She's gone away to school.''

''School?'' Zach asked softly, looking at Susan.

''She's a freshman at the University of Nebraska.''

''Damn it! We're being married tonight. Don't you think you could've told me these things earlier?'' He felt like he'd been blindsided.

This time she looked at him. Then she coolly asked, ''What difference does it make?''

Her question stumped him. She was right. Her family information would have no affect on him. This marriage wasn't real. So why did it bother him?

''Gramp thinks Paul is your son.''

''He is,'' Susan said, with a smile over her shoulder directed toward her little brother. ''I helped take care of him since his birth, and four years ago, I became his mother."

He tightened his grip on the wheel. Somehow those words didn't fit into the picture he had created of Susan. Beautiful, self-centered, greedy. She was too beautiful for her own good. But he could resist surface beauty. What was he going to do if he found out she was beautiful inside, too?

Susan held on to Paul's hand as they approached the hospital room. In the car, when Zach had been questioning her, she'd been calm. But now that the moment for their bizarre plan had arrived, she was shaking inside.

"You're squeezing my hand," Paul complained, tugging.

"Sorry, sweetie. Be sure and don't tell anyone our secret, okay?"

"I won't. Will Zach be my daddy?"

That was the reason she hadn't wanted Paul involved in this. She didn't want him thinking he had a father. She leaned down and kissed his cheek. "Sort of. But not really."

Paul looked at her as if she were speaking a foreign language. "Huh?"

"We'll talk about it later."

Zach held open the door. "Ready?" he whispered.

"What about the license?" she suddenly asked. "I didn't fill out any forms."

"We've got it taken care of. You'll have to fill in

a few blanks, but a friend of Gramp's, a judge, arranged everything.''

Then he led the way into the hospital room.

Three men dressed in dark suits were standing by the bed. Zach shook their hands before he turned to his grandfather.

''Gramp? We're here.''

''Good, boy. Introduce Susan to them. Paul? You there?''

Paul had no hesitation about going to Pete Lowery's side, and Susan barely listened to the introductions as she tried to keep an eye on Paul.

The minister, the judge Zach had previously mentioned, and the doctor greeted her politely.

''Let's get this show on the road,'' Pete said from his bed, holding Paul's hand. ''Me and my new great-grandson want to celebrate.''

Paul leaned over toward him. ''Can I call you Gramp?''

Susan's heart cracked at the enthusiasm in Paul's voice. She shouldn't have given in to Zach's demand that Paul be included. He was going to be so hurt when Pete died and Zach was no longer around.

''A'course you can. What else would you call me?'' The old man beamed at Paul.

She felt Zach's gaze on her, but she refused to look at him. She just wanted the evening to be over.

The minister stepped forward. ''I think we're ready to begin. If you two will step forward,'' he said with a kindly smile.

''Get the flowers,'' Pete called from the bed.

"I almost forgot," the judge replied and went to the closet in the room. He brought out a beautiful bouquet of creamy roses with the faintest tinge of pink in them. Handing them to Susan, he offered her a courtly bow.

"Thank you so much. They're beautiful." She gave the man her first real smile of the evening.

"Pete remembered. He's the one you should thank."

She moved to the side of the bed where Paul stood and bent over him to kiss Pete's cheek. "Thank you, Mr. Lowery. The flowers are beautiful."

"Not as beautiful as you, girl. And no calling me Mr., either. I'll be Gramp to both of you."

She gave him a smile but felt it wobbling. She hurried back to the minister's side, hoping Pete hadn't noticed.

Zach was waiting for her.

Shivers swept over her. What was she doing? How could she have agreed to this marriage? She closed her eyes.

Was she going to faint?

Zach reached out and took her hand. She'd been acting strangely all evening, as if this pretense was bothering her. He hadn't expected a woman with a conscience. Or was she just a good actress?

She opened her eyes and stared at him. Zach breathed a sigh of relief and nodded to the minister.

"Dearly beloved, we are gathered here…"

They proceeded through the ceremony until the

minister asked for the rings. Susan gasped, obviously thinking he'd forgotten such an important thing. He'd been busy all day long, preparing for this evening.

He reached in the pocket of his tux and handed two rings to the minister. His was a plain gold band. Hers was a band covered with two carats of diamonds.

When the minister bid him to do so, he slid the band on her finger. He'd guessed at the size, and it was a little large.

Susan stared at the ring, seeming to lose track of where she was. He nudged her when she didn't respond to the minister's words. She jerked her head up and stared at him.

"My ring," he whispered.

She finally reached for the ring the minister was holding out and placed it on his finger, repeating the words. Her voice and her fingers were trembling.

"I now pronounce you man and wife," the minister said. "You may kiss the bride."

Susan swung her gaze to him, her eyes wide with surprise. Fortunately Gramp couldn't see her face. Zach pulled her into his arms and lowered his lips to hers.

He'd only intended a brief brushing of their lips, as he'd done the night before. But her trembling body, pressed against his, distracted him. His lips covered hers and found an excitement even greater than last night. As if protesting, she opened her lips against his and he deepened the kiss, until he almost forgot they had an audience. His hands slid down the silk dress, learning her curves, wanting more.

"All right, already, boy. Don't eat her alive," Pete ordered from the bed.

He broke away, almost dropping Susan, who looked dazed. He grabbed her again as she sagged against him. "Are you okay?"

"Yes." She drew a deep breath. "Yes, of course."

"Congratulations, Mrs. Lowery," the judge said, offering his hand. She blinked several times before she accepted his handshake. The minister and the doctor followed with their congratulations.

Zach shook their hands, too, but all he could think about was getting Susan back into his arms. Their kiss had stirred him more than any kiss ever had. He was having difficulty returning to reality.

"All right. Let's party!" Pete called from the bed. "Doc, did you arrange everything?"

"Yes, but you have to keep your promise."

"Paul and I will drink mineral water, right, boy? We don't need any of that nasty champagne."

"What's champagne?" Paul asked.

"Stuff you won't like. But the cake, ah, you'll love the cake. And you have to eat my piece, too, 'cause I promised that mean man over there that I wouldn't eat any."

"Not even a bite?" Paul asked, seeing the tragedy of that promise.

"It's okay."

Zach took Susan's hand and pulled her over to the bed. "What are you talking about, Gramp? You need to stay quiet."

"Don't be silly, boy. The doc approved everything."

The doctor stepped to Zach's side. "Your grandfather wanted to celebrate your marriage, Mr. Lowery. He promised to behave himself, and he does seem to be feeling better."

The door opened and a nurse pushed a hospital cart into the room. A small wedding cake, exquisitely decorated, along with plates and forks, was on it, as well as a bottle of champagne and a bottle of mineral water.

"But I didn't expect... Gramp, you should've been resting, not planning a party," Zach protested.

To his surprise, Susan, who had appeared on the verge of fainting two minutes ago, stepped forward to kiss his grandfather's cheek again. "I think it's very sweet of you, Gramp."

"Good girl. Raise my bed a little more and bring Paul and me some mineral water. We want to toast the bride and groom, don't we, Paul?"

"Yeah."

Zach grinned. The kid had no idea what Gramp meant, but he'd go along with anything tonight.

"All right, two mineral waters coming up." He poured the water, finding glasses on the bottom shelf of the cart. Then he opened the champagne, making Susan jump when the cork came out. He poured glasses for everyone else, then turned to his grandfather. "Okay, Gramp. The toast is yours."

The old man lifted his glass and motioned for Paul

to do the same. "To Zach and Susan. May they have a long, happy marriage, with lots of little ones."

Everyone sipped.

"This boy wants some cake," Gramp ordered. "Susan, you and Zach should cut the first piece."

Zach wasn't going to argue. He knew how this part worked. It meant he got a chance to put his arms around Susan again.

He closed his hands over hers around the knife and pretended great interest in cutting the cake.

Until his grandfather spoke again.

"Where are you two going on your honeymoon?"

Chapter Four

Zach choked on the bite of cake he'd just put in his mouth.

The judge gave him several whacks on his back. When he recovered, his first thought was Susan. She was almost as pale as her gown, staring at him with huge blue eyes.

"Uh, Gramp, we're putting the honeymoon off for a while."

Color flooded into Susan's cheeks. "We want to concentrate on your getting well, Gramp. That's the most important thing."

"Well, now, I figured that's what you'd say, so I made a few plans of my own." The old man looked quite pleased with himself.

"Gramp, I refuse to leave town until you're better," Zach insisted, in spite of the temptation a honeymoon with the beautiful woman next to him held.

"That's why I rented the honeymoon suite at the Plaza Hotel. It's just a few blocks away. The manager is a close friend, and he's promised me you'll have the best service."

"But Gramp," Susan said, her words breathless, as if she, too, were thinking about them being alone, "I have Paul. I can't—"

"I can stay at Rosa's," Paul said. "Then I can show Manny my new books." He turned to Pete. "Zach bought me some books about a dog."

"Good for him. You don't mind staying with this Rosa? 'Cause the doc said you could go to his house," Pete said.

"I'd like to go to Rosa's. Manny's my friend."

"That okay with you, Susan?" Pete asked, smiling at her.

Zach sympathized with her. It wasn't the first time his grandfather had maneuvered people into doing what he wanted. But it was a new experience for Susan.

"Yes, of course, that will be fine," Susan said hurriedly. "It's very thoughtful of you, Gramp. A—a night in such a beautiful hotel will be quite...quite charming."

"One night? You think I'm a cheapskate? I want you to stay through the weekend."

"Zach?" she pleaded in a soft whisper.

"We can't leave Paul that long, Gramp. We'll go tonight, but after that, we'll have to make arrangements...about a lot of things."

"Well, I can't force you. But the boy would be fine at the ranch with Hester. You like animals, boy?"

Paul's eyes widened. "Animals? You mean, like dogs? I don't have a dog 'cause we can't have one at the apartment. I always wanted a dog."

Susan covered her face with one hand. Zach didn't know if it was because she felt bad about the boy not having a dog, or what. But he believed little boys and dogs were meant to be together.

"We have several dogs, Paul. You'll like them," Gramp assured him.

"Wow! Wait until I tell Manny!"

"It's about time for the party to end," the doctor said quietly, moving to Pete's side.

"All right," he agreed, which worried Zach. "I'm going to get a report from the manager at the hotel, so you two enjoy yourselves," he added with a grin.

"We'll do our best, Gramp," Zach promised, unable to help himself. He caught Susan's sharp stare out of the corner of his eye and turned to smile reassuringly. She didn't appear to be comforted.

"Doctor, Reverend Knox, Judge, thanks for helping Gramp pull off this celebration. It meant a lot to him," Zach said as he shook each man's hand. He noticed how graciously Susan added her thanks.

Then she turned to his grandfather, giving him a kiss on each cheek. "Thank you for making this evening memorable, Gramp."

"You're welcome, little girl. And welcome to the family, both of you." He beamed at Susan and Paul.

Zach stepped up, putting his arm around Susan. He

hoped Gramp didn't notice her start of surprise. "Thanks, Gramp. You're the best."

"Aw, go on with you, boy."

They left the room, with Gramp smiling, even when the nurse brought in his medicine.

"Will Rosa mind letting Paul spend the night?" Zach asked after they'd driven several blocks.

"Surely that isn't necessary? You can check into the hotel and—"

"Didn't you hear Gramp say the manager is a friend? He'd tell Gramp I lost my bride and then there'd be hell to pay."

"Oh, you said a bad word," Paul said from the back seat. He was holding his new books, rubbing his hand over them, as if afraid they'd disappear if he wasn't touching them.

"Sorry, buddy, I forgot," Zach said good-naturedly. Then, as if he hadn't been interrupted, he said, "So it's all settled."

Susan crossed her arms, hoping it would keep Zach from noticing her trembling fingers. "Have you noticed how everything is always settled your way?"

He took the wind out of her sails with his quiet response. "How would you like to settle things, Susan? I thought you didn't want to hurt Gramp."

"Of course I don't want to hurt him! He's such a dear!"

"He said I could call him Gramp," Paul said from the back seat with great satisfaction. "Now I have a grandfather. Can I tell Manny?"

Susan moaned, trying to think how to answer.

Zach didn't hesitate. "Of course you can, buddy."

Gasping, Susan turned to glare at him. In a fierce whisper, she said, "Paul is mine! Not yours! I make the decisions about him and don't you forget it."

He met her glare with a cool stare before turning his attention back to his driving. Nothing more was said until he parked the car by her apartment.

"Is there anything I can do to help you pack for tonight?"

"No! Nothing. Come on, Paul." She opened her door and helped Paul out. She hoped Zach would remain in the car, but she should've known better. He was right behind them as they went up the stairs.

"Put on your pajamas and gather up clean clothes for tomorrow, sweetie," she ordered Paul, suddenly feeling tired. "I'll go talk to Rosa."

Ignoring Zach, she opened her front door and crossed to Rosa's door. By the time she'd finished explaining the need for her brother to stay over, Paul was beside her, carrying his new books, excitement on his face.

"Can I stay, Rosa?"

"Of course you can. Manny is getting ready for bed."

"I got new books about a dog!" he said as he scooted underneath Rosa's arm.

"What about a good-night hug for me?" Susan called. Her brother spun around, raced back to hug her, then ran off again.

Rosa laughed, then sobered. "You okay?"

"I'm fine. I'll be here tomorrow at the regular time."

"All right. Have a nice night."

Susan stood on the landing, taking a deep breath after Rosa closed her door. Yeah, right. A nice night. Finally, she opened the door to her apartment, finding Zach standing in the middle of the living room, waiting.

Without a word, she walked into her room. The only suitcase she had was an old, scuffed overnight bag, but she couldn't exactly use a paper sack, so she dragged it out of the back of her closet. It took only a couple of minutes to put in what she'd need for tomorrow.

When she came out with the bag in her hand, Zach stepped forward to take it. After getting a good look at what he was carrying, he looked at her, one brow slipping up in question.

Her cheeks red, she said, "That's all I have."

With a gentle smile, he said, "It's more than I've got, so don't worry about it."

His kindness eased her embarrassment.

Susan had never stayed in a hotel room before. She didn't want to confess such inexperience. Things were scary enough without having to deal with Zach's scorn. So she followed him into the brightly lit, elegantly decorated lobby.

He waved aside the bellboy's offer to take her suitcase and approached the check-in counter. To her surprise, the lady behind the counter greeted him by name.

"Good evening, Mr. Lowery. We have your new key all ready, and we've transferred your belongings to your new room."

"Oh, thank you. I was going to ask about that," he said with a smile, but Susan was beginning to know him and saw a tenseness in his posture.

"I won't need your key back. We've already changed the code on the door."

"Right. Well, we'll just go on up."

"Of course. And call if you need anything." Then the woman shifted her gaze to Susan. "Congratulations, Mrs. Lowery."

"Thank you," Susan murmured, trying to present a proper bridal air.

Zach took her hand and started toward the elevator.

"Is everything all right?" she asked softly.

"Later."

They rode in silence to the top floor. When they got off, Susan noted there were only two doors. Zach moved to the door on his right, pulling her along behind him.

He slid the key in the door just as the second elevator door slid open. A waiter got off, pushing a cart. "Good evening, Mr. and Mrs. Lowery. Mr. Peter Lowery ordered a surprise for you."

"Great," Zach muttered. He pushed open the door. "Go ahead."

"Certainly, sir. That way I can hold open the door for you to carry your bride over the threshold."

Susan tried to cover her gasp with her hand. When she looked at Zach, she read the answer to her unspoken question. Yes, he would be carrying her over the threshold.

He set down her small bag and reached for her. He swung her up into the air with an ease she admired. The man was strong, as Paul had said.

The waiter beamed at them, seeming to wait for something else. When Zach's lips covered hers, she knew what it was. And discovered that the kiss at their wedding wasn't a fluke. When this man touched her, she seemed to lose control. Her head was spinning when he slid her down his body.

That didn't reduce the excitement racing through her body.

Immediately, the waiter removed several domed lids to reveal Gramp's present, an array of cheeses, crackers and a beautiful pile of chocolate-dipped strawberries, along with another bottle of champagne.

Then he bowed and waited for Zach's tip.

Susan turned away, hoping to hide her excitement...and her fear.

That's when she saw the room she had entered. Or rather, the suite. The beautiful living room had a wall of windows looking over Kansas City. It opened into an elegant dining room. She assumed the door on the nearest wall was the bedroom. She thought her entire apartment was smaller than just the living room and dining room.

The snap of the door closing behind the waiter had her spinning around. "It's so big."

"Not big enough."

She stared at him, wondering how spoiled he must be to need more space. "How can you say that?"

"Because it's only got one bed, Susan. Unless you've decided you want to share, that's going to be a problem."

Her cheeks flamed. "Oh."

"That's why I was upset. I hadn't thought about the fact they would automatically move my clothes and cancel my room. I guess I had too much on my mind."

"Oh," she repeated, unable to think of anything to say. Then, she said, "The couch is a big one. I'll sleep there."

"No," he said with a sigh, "I'll take the couch."

"But I'm shorter than you. It will be more—"

"Susan!" he snapped. "I'll take the couch!" He stomped away from her without waiting for an answer. At the dining table, where the waiter had placed the food, he began filling a plate.

"You're hungry?"

"No. But Gramp will get a report on whether or not we enjoyed his gift. Come eat something."

As she reluctantly filled a plate, he opened the bottle of champagne and poured two glasses.

"I—I don't usually drink," she said shakily.

He smiled at her, which increased his attractiveness.

She sighed.

"And you already had a glass at the wedding?" he asked.

"Well, a couple of sips only."

"You're a high roller, aren't you, Susan?" His smile sharpened.

"I don't know what you mean."

"Nothing. I was teasing. Want to sit down?"

"I'd rather just go to bed," she whispered. When his eyes lit up, she realized her mistake. "Alone! I meant alone."

"I was afraid that was what you meant. Can't you eat a little more?"

She removed more domed lids and looked at stuffed mushrooms, chicken wings, deviled eggs, and she sighed. "I—I suppose."

He put his plate and glass on the table and crossed to her. "Don't worry about it. I'll tell Gramp I kept you too busy to eat." He took the plate from her hand.

"Oh." The meaning of his words brought the blood to her cheeks again. "Thank you." And she rushed into the bedroom, only to stop and stare at the huge bed, the covers turned back and chocolate mints on the pillows.

"Oh," she said, staring.

"Is that the only word you know?" he demanded, arriving behind her with her suitcase in his hand.

"I've never...it's beautiful."

"You've never stayed in a suite before?"

"I've never stayed in a hotel before," she whispered.

He set the bag down beside the bed. "I'm sorry. Well, you're starting at the top. This is a great hotel."

"You've stayed in this suite before?"

He rolled his eyes. "Not exactly. This is the bridal suite, honey."

"But you've been married before," she reminded him. Somehow the thought of him occupying this suite with his ex-wife was painful, though she couldn't explain why.

"We went to Paris for our honeymoon," he said, his voice rough, as if the memory was unpleasant. He crossed over to the closet and pulled a blanket from the shelf. "Mind if I take a pillow?"

"Of course not. Do you need more covers?"

"No. And there's a bathroom on the other side of the kitchen, so I won't need to bother you again tonight." He strode past her, but just as she released her pent-up breath, he stopped and dipped his head, brushing his lips across hers.

It wasn't the knockout kiss from the wedding, or the kiss they'd shared when he'd carried her across the threshold. But it was sweet. Tender and sweet.

The growl in his voice told her he didn't think so.

"Good night!"

Damn! He'd barely escaped the bedroom without breaking his word. He'd promised Susan their marriage would be on her terms. He hadn't realized how difficult that promise would be to keep.

Susan was a beautiful woman. But when she'd confessed she'd never been in a hotel room before, he'd wanted to cuddle her against him and tell her he'd make her first experience one to remember.

He wanted to share a first with her.

What had started out as a simple scheme to please Gramp had become quite complicated.

"Zach?"

Her soft voice had him spinning around. She was hiding behind the bedroom door, but he could see enough of her attire to realize she was dressed in a plain white T-shirt.

"Yeah?"

"Um, I need to be at work at eight-thirty in the morning."

"Call in sick."

She reacted as if he'd suggested she rob a bank. "I can't do that!"

"Susan, it's your honeymoon!"

"We both know it's not. Besides, you're the one who decided to get married on a Tuesday night. I have to go to work. Will you wake me up?"

"Dial 0 on the phone and ask for a wake-up call. They'll give you one whatever time you want it."

"Thank you."

The door closed and he was alone in the room again. With a mental picture of Susan in a white T-shirt. He immediately wondered how long the shirt was. It shouldn't have been sexy. Most brides wore elegant peignoirs—lace, satin…nothing.

Susan in a white T-shirt.

He groaned and picked up his glass of champagne. After downing its contents, he filled the glass again, picked up his plate of food, turned on the television and sat down on the couch.

It was going to be a long night.

Susan woke when the phone rang. She answered at once, hoping it hadn't disturbed Zach. After hanging up, she sank back against the pillows, reluctant to leave the most comfortable bed she'd ever experienced.

With a sigh, she shoved back the covers. In the luxurious bath, she showered and dressed, then gathered up her belongings. After carefully making the big bed, she picked up her bag and paused at the door.

Her reason for being there wasn't what she wished it was, but it had still been an enjoyable experience. Once Zach left the room.

She eased open the door and tiptoed past the sofa, staring at him as he lay sprawled on the long sofa. The blanket was pulled up to his chest but not over it. And his chest was bare.

She drew a deep breath, staring at his hard muscles, the dark hair that covered the broad expanse of skin. He could pose for those male calendars if he ever needed money.

Oh, yeah, *that* was going to happen.

Backing away from the sofa before she could be tempted to touch him, she bumped into the door. She stared at him, scarcely breathing. When he didn't move, she hurriedly undid the lock and turned the knob, easing the door open.

Once she was in the hall, with her bag in her hand and the door closed, she breathed a sigh of relief. When the elevator pinged after she'd pushed the button, she wanted to shush it, but then she realized how silly her reaction was.

She was feeling good about her escape until she was crossing the lobby.

"Mrs. Lowery?"

The waiter from last night had been talking to one of the bellboys when he'd spotted her.

"Is everything all right?"

"Oh, yes! Yes, but I have to go to work and—oh, no!"

"What is it?"

"I don't have my car here. I forgot." What was she going to do now? She wasn't sure she had enough money to pay for a taxi.

"The hotel van will take you wherever you want to go," the waiter said, as if her request was normal.

"Really? That would be wonderful."

"Wait right here."

In no time, the waiter escorted her to the door and introduced her to a young man in a similar uniform. He opened the passenger door to a shuttle van for her, then circled the van and slid behind the wheel.

"Where do you need to go? The airport?"

"No. The Lucky Charm Diner on Wornall."

"Hey, I know that place. Good food."

She smiled. It was a short drive, and the driver chatted about the weather and the sports teams, relieving Susan of any need to talk.

When she walked into the diner, her tension eased. Slipping through the kitchen, she greeted the chefs and hurried into her office, hiding her suitcase under the desk.

The door opened and Kate stuck her head in. "Hi. How's everything going?"

"Great. I'm a little late—"

"Don't be silly. I'm going to be here all morning, so if you have any questions for the brochure, let me know." She almost pulled the door closed, then opened it again. "By the way, Nathan can count to ten now." Nathan was Kate's little boy.

Susan smiled. "He's a genius!"

"I know. You and Paul want to come to dinner tonight? We haven't seen you much lately."

"That would be nice," she agreed at once. Paul always enjoyed their visits to Kate or Maggie's homes.

She settled down to work after Kate returned to the kitchen. It felt good to ignore the bizarre events of the past two nights and concentrate on her work.

No one bothered her until almost eleven. Then Kate opened the door again.

"Hi, Kate. Are you leaving?" Usually her half sister only put in half a day at the diner.

"No, not yet. Uh, Susan, there's a man on the telephone. He says he's your husband. Is there something you haven't told me?"

Chapter Five

Zach drummed his fingers on the bedside table as he waited for Susan to come to the phone. Not only had she left without awakening him, she'd made the damn bed!

Room service had delivered breakfast a few minutes ago, ordered by his grandfather. Zach had had the forethought to throw the pillow into the bedroom, wrap the blanket around his waist as a makedo robe and fluff up the pillows on the couch. The waiter had offered to serve their breakfast to them in bed, but he'd firmly refused.

It wasn't any thanks to Susan that disaster had been averted. Then he'd called the diner and was given the third degree by some woman before she'd call Susan to the phone.

He wasn't a happy camper.

"Zach?"

Her hesitancy bothered him even more. He barked into the receiver, "Do you have some other husband I don't know about?"

Silence.

He tried again. "Why didn't you wake me before you left? I felt like a fool waking up with you gone and room service knocking on the door."

"I thought you'd want to sleep."

Her response was thoughtful, especially since he'd been up half the night thinking about her and her virginal T-shirt, wondering if she'd worn her bra under... He forced his thoughts to a screeching halt. "We need to make plans."

"About what?"

"Seeing Gramp, for one thing. He'll expect us to come visit him together."

"No, we can't," she replied with a muffled voice, sending his temper through the roof.

"Look, I paid good money—"

"No, not you!"

"What's going on, Susan? You're driving me crazy."

"That was my sister you talked to," she told him. "She wants us to come for dinner tonight." Her voice grew more distant, as if she'd turned her head away from the receiver. "I'd forgotten, Kate. We have to go to the hospital."

"You just said..." Zach protested.

"Oh. Zach, my sister wants us to come to their house at six for—for dinner."

Zach knit his brow. "I'm confused. What am I supposed to say?"

"His grandfather will be expecting us." Pause. "Yes, he's in intensive care." Pause. "You're right, of course. I guess there would be time to eat, but we don't want to put you to any trouble."

Zach held the phone, listening, but he didn't bother to answer. She was having a conversation with her sister. Suddenly it occurred to him that the only sister she'd mentioned was Megan, an eighteen-year-old, away at school.

"How is Megan going to fix dinner for us? I thought she was in Nebraska."

"Not Megan. Kate," she told him. Then her voice was muffled again. "Yes, I guess we can. Is six o'clock okay with you?"

He listened.

"Zach? Are you there?"

"Hell, yes, I'm here, but it's hard to tell when you're talking to me and when you aren't."

"I'm talking to you. Can we have dinner at my sister's at six o'clock? Then they'll baby-sit Paul for us."

"Am I supposed to say yes?"

"Of course. Zach says thank you, Kate. We'll be there at six."

"Are you ready to talk to me now?" he asked impatiently. "I think I should take you out to lunch so we can get things straightened out. I'll pick you up in fifteen minutes."

"I have lunch between eleven-thirty and twelve."

Who did she work for, a slave driver? "That's criminal. Everyone gets an hour for lunch."

"Um, okay, today I'll take an hour."

"Right. Be ready."

Susan reluctantly hung up the phone. She knew what awaited her. Kate would grill her until she knew every last detail of her "marriage." She faced her sister, drawing a deep breath.

To her surprise, Kate ignored her, reaching for the phone. After dialing, she spoke into the phone. "Maggie? Can you come to the diner right now? Susan got married, and she's about to tell me why we weren't invited. I didn't think you'd want to miss the explanation."

After waiting for Maggie's response, Kate hung up the phone and turned to stare at Susan. "Any complaints? This way you'll only have to explain once."

Susan reluctantly grinned. She should've known. Kate and Maggie were very close. Since she'd met them eighteen months ago, the three of them had been building a friendship that meant so much to her. But Kate would always include Maggie.

And she was right. This way Susan would only have to explain the humiliating situation she was in one time. "I hope she hurries. Zach said he'd be here in fifteen minutes, and he didn't sound in an accommodating mood."

Kate raised her chin, her red hair framing her determined face. "He can wait."

Somehow, Kate's reaction raised Susan's spirits.

Since she'd gotten involved in Zach's problems, it seemed he'd run roughshod over her, through no fault of his own. But it felt good to have someone on her side.

"I'll get us all a cup of coffee," she said, knowing to take it to the back booth, where she'd first served Zach. That booth was the traditional family booth. Only used for customers when the diner was full.

Maggie arrived in five minutes. She was a quiet brunette, steady and calm to Kate's flash and dash. Susan worried about explaining to Maggie, because she wasn't impulsive like Kate. Except once.

Maybe she would understand, after all.

"You're married?" Maggie asked as she slid into the booth across from Susan.

"Not really."

Kate raised one eyebrow as she joined them. "That man clearly said you were his wife."

"There was a ceremony, but it's not real."

"I think you'd better explain," Maggie ordered.

Susan tried to remember all the intricacies of the past two days.

"You needed money and didn't come to us?" Kate demanded, partway through.

"Kate, I know you've offered, but Megan and Paul are my responsibilities. And I still have to pay some of Mom's debts off. I can't ask you—"

"I know. You're hardheaded. Go on."

When Susan had finished, Kate and Maggie stared at each other, then looked back at her.

"What happens now?" Kate asked.

"I don't know. I mean, we have to keep pretending until…until there isn't any need." That question had occurred to Susan several times that morning, when she'd let down her guard.

"You mean until his grandfather dies," Maggie said.

"Yes. But he's the dearest man. It's so hard to think about… I mean, I can't hope for him to die!"

"No, of course not," Kate agreed, "but what about Zach? What's he like?"

"What difference does that make?" Susan asked, uneasy about answering. She didn't want her sisters to know about the attraction she felt.

"Will he keep his word?" Maggie asked.

"Of course I will, if you're talking about me," Zach said.

Susan gasped. She faced the door, but she'd been so involved in the telling of her problems, she'd forgotten to watch for him.

"Want to scoot over, honey?" he said, sliding into the booth even as she did so.

Well, one thing was clear. The attraction hadn't gone away. He was back in tight jeans and a plaid shirt today, his Stetson in place. She sat up as he promptly removed his hat and ran a big hand through his dark hair.

"Now, I don't want you to think I don't have any manners, so I'll just tell you that Susan only mentioned Megan, who's in Nebraska. I didn't know she had other sisters." With a nod, he said, "I'm Zach Lowery."

Kate and Maggie introduced themselves. Then Kate asked, "Of the Lowery ranch?"

"Yep. Susan didn't tell you?"

"I didn't mention your last name," Susan said, staring at the table. "There wasn't much time."

"We're Susan's half sisters, actually," Maggie explained. "We've only known about each other for a year and a half."

"I'm pleased to meet both of you. And I will keep my word to Susan. She's doing me a big favor."

Kate frowned and opened her mouth, but Susan forestalled her. "Kate, I'm a big girl. Everything's going to be just fine."

"I know, but—"

"No, Kate, I don't want to discuss that now," Susan hurriedly said, knowing somehow that Kate was going to talk about money and her finances. She certainly didn't want Zach to know anything about her situation.

Maggie supported her, much to Susan's relief. "She's right, Kate. We can get together and discuss those other problems when we have time. Zach and Susan probably want to spend some time alone."

Susan's cheeks flooded with color. Zach was going to think she was pursuing him. "Yes, to plan our visits to the hospital. We have to coordinate a few things, that's all."

Zach nodded, lifted his hat to his head and slid from the booth. "So, you're ready to go to lunch?"

"Yes." She stood, too, eager to escape from Kate's questions. And even more from the gentle understanding in Maggie's eyes. She seemed to know Susan was attracted to the man beside her.

"You could eat here. On the house," Kate added.

Zach clenched his jaw, as if she'd insulted him. "Thanks, but I've already made reservations."

"Then we'll see you tonight. Susan knows the way," Kate returned, staring back at him.

"Damn it, how much more family do you have?" he demanded as soon as they were in his rental car.

"That's it, except for their husbands. Oh, and they have three darling children between them."

"Didn't you explain to them that the marriage isn't real? That we signed an agreement?"

"Yes, of course I did," she protested.

"Then why were they vetting me? I didn't expect that." And he didn't much like it. The redhead, Kate, had looked at him as if she didn't trust him.

"I didn't expect anyone to tell them," Susan retorted, anger in her voice. "If you hadn't decided to announce to the world that we were married, it wouldn't have happened."

He didn't have anything else to say. He was guilty. But the woman had been reluctant to call Susan to the phone. Okay, so he'd been impatient. He wasn't used to people telling him no.

He particularly didn't like being told no in regard to the woman beside him. He was having to tell himself no often enough. No, to touching her. No, to claiming her as his own. No, to taking her to bed.

Why should he have to put up with a no from someone else?

He parked the car outside an expensive restaurant on the Plaza, the famous outdoor shopping mall in Kansas City. No words were spoken as they entered the restaurant and an attentive waiter showed them to a table.

He waited until they'd ordered before he spoke again. "Look, Susan, let's put all this family stuff aside. There's no point in arguing over things that don't matter." He drew a breath of relief when she nodded in agreement.

"Okay. I'm going to the hospital after lunch. Then I'll pick you up at your place at— I don't know how far it is to your sister's house."

"Not far. About fifteen minutes."

"Where do they live?"

"Near the Plaza."

He frowned. "Pretty pricey digs. They have a lot of money?"

"Why?"

Damn it, the woman was staring at him with a suspicious expression on her face. "Just curious. Did you think I was planning a robbery or something?"

She shrugged her shoulders and looked away, sinking her teeth into her bottom lip. "So…so you'll pick me up around five-thirty or a little after?" She started to get up.

"Yeah. Where are you going? We haven't eaten yet."

"Oh. I—I forgot," she whispered, revealing her nervousness.

He reached out and covered her hand with his, feeling it tremble. "Hey, sunshine, quit worrying. You're doing a good thing. I've already talked to Gramp this morning. He's feeling better than he has the entire past six months."

She nodded and tugged on her hand.

"Any problems at work this morning?"

She seemed surprised by his question. "No, of course not."

"How long have you worked there?"

"Just a little over a week."

The waitress brought their food, but Zach didn't let the conversation drop. In no time, he'd wormed the information out of her about her previous job and the sexual harassment she'd suffered.

"Hey, they've got laws against that!"

"Yes, but I need a salary coming in. I couldn't afford to fight that battle."

There was no whining or self-pity. Just a matter-of-fact explanation. He hated the thought that some man had treated her so badly, but he understood why it had happened. She was beautiful. More than beautiful, she gave the appearance of something gentle and...and precious. Strange word for him to use, but it described her.

"Well, at least you know that won't happen now, working for your sister."

"Yes, I'm quite lucky."

None of the women he'd dated—or married—

would consider herself lucky to live in a run-down apartment supporting two siblings. Another interesting thought.

"We'd better hurry. I need to be back at work."

"A half hour for lunch is ridiculous."

"No, I requested it. That way I get home earlier for Paul. I like to have as much time as possible with him."

"Say, I forgot, but after I visit with Gramp, can I pick Paul up? I've got a few things to do that I think he'd enjoy." He waited for her response, unsure whether she'd trust him with her beloved little brother.

"There's no need—"

"Susan, I *want* to. In fact, we might even invite Manuel along, too. Paul seems to enjoy his friend."

"Yes, they're like brothers. If you're sure you want both of them, I'll give Rosa a call."

"Yeah, do that."

Pete Lowery was sitting up in bed when Zach got to the hospital. "Gramp, you're looking good."

"Yep. I've surprised the doctors. They thought I was a goner." He beamed at his grandson.

Zach muttered beneath his breath. "Me, too." Fortunately, while Gramp's heart may have recovered, his hearing was still slightly off. "Glad to hear it," Zach added.

"You enjoyed the hotel suite?"

"You bet. Susan loved it."

"She's a sweet thing. How did you find her?"

Zach drew a deep breath. "Well, I stopped off at this diner one day, when I'd come to town to check with our banker, and she served me coffee."

"She's a waitress?"

"Nope. She works in public relations for the diner, and when she gets coffee for herself, she sometimes helps the waitress out by refilling everyone else's cups."

"Public relations? I bet she draws a lot of attention."

"Yeah."

"Where is she?"

"At work."

Pete glared at him. "You gonna make your bride a slave? She shouldn't have to work the day after her wedding."

Zach decided to let Susan bear the blame for this one. "I told her that, but since we hadn't planned on marrying this soon, she said she couldn't leave them in the lurch. She's very responsible."

"The minute she starts a baby, you make sure she stays at home and is taken care of. We don't want anything to go wrong."

Zach rolled his eyes. "Gramp, I know how to take care of what's mine. Susan and I are coming back to see you tonight, after we have dinner with more of her family that I just met. But I have to go now. I'm taking Paul shopping." He leaned over and patted his grandfather's shoulder.

Then he remembered something else he'd better straighten out while he had a chance. "Oh, by the way, Paul is her brother, not her son. And she has an eighteen-year-old sister named Megan. She's been trying to support them the last four years.''

''She's a good girl,'' Pete said simply, still beaming at Zach.

He nodded and left the hospital room. He hoped Gramp was right. But he still wasn't sure.

The next few hours, he had more fun than he'd had in a long time. After picking up Paul and Manuel, he headed for the stores. The two little boys were astounded when they discovered they were to be treated to new clothes.

Zach did run into a little trouble when he suggested Paul and Manuel each choose several shirts.

''I don't think we should buy more than one shirt,'' Paul said, his blue eyes serious.

''Why not, buddy?''

''I don't think Susan would want me to.''

Zach frowned. ''Why not? Doesn't she like you to have nice clothes?''

''Yeah, but when Aunt Kate or Aunt Maggie want to buy me lots of things, Susan says just one, please.''

Zach wanted to dismiss Paul's worry, but the little boy's serious face made him reconsider. ''Okay, how about I buy you one pair of jeans and a shirt and shoes and, uh, maybe a cowboy hat for when you come out to the ranch, and Gramp buys you the other stuff.''

Paul thought Zach's idea was a brilliant one, but then they had to deal with Manuel's concerns about strangers buying him things, too. Zach couldn't remember working so hard to spend money. Once he'd satisfied both boys' consciences, they made more rapid progress.

He particularly enjoyed buying them cowboy boots and hats.

"But I won't be going to visit the ranch," Manuel whispered to Paul.

"Paul may want to invite you," Zach said, having overheard the anxious whisper. "Wouldn't you like to come with Paul? Don't you like horses and cows?"

Manuel beamed at him. "I love 'em. Paul said you had puppies, too."

"Oh, yeah. We've got puppies, and I think they love little boys." He was rewarded with big grins. Ruffling first one boy's hair and then the other's, he decided he could get used to having kids around.

"You know, by next month, it may be a little cold out on the ranch. I think we'd better check out those windbreakers over there, too."

Now that he'd convinced them there would be no problem with Susan and Rosa, the boys entered into the spirit of the shopping spree.

"This is even better than Christmas," Paul said, squeezing the packages against his little chest. "Can we buy something for Susan? She doesn't usually get presents 'cause me and Megan don't have much money."

"That's a good idea, Paul," Zach said. He wasn't sure Susan would appreciate anything from him, but every bride should have a present. And Gramp would expect it.

Since there was nothing in the children's department for Susan, they swung by the jewelry counter. Zach, with both boys' taste consulted, decided on a diamond tennis bracelet that would sparkle on Susan's delicate wrist.

Then they loaded all their packages in the trunk of his car and headed for the apartment. Once there, they reversed the procedure. Each boy carried several packages, but Zach bore the brunt of the shopping.

Susan was already home. She came out on the landing as they started up the stairs.

"There you are. We've been worried—" she broke off, her eyes widening as she saw the packages. "Good heavens, what have you done?"

Chapter Six

Susan couldn't believe her eyes. Even the boys were loaded down with packages. She waited for an answer to her question.

"A little shopping," Zach said easily. "I thought the boys needed a few things."

"It's okay, Susan," Paul hurriedly said. "Zach only bought us one of everything. Gramp bought the other ones."

She struggled to compose herself. Since Zach had taken it upon himself to purchase clothes for her brother and his friend, she'd have to deduct that amount from the check he'd given her and repay him. She only hoped he'd been practical.

"I see. And did you enjoy yourselves?" she asked, smiling at the boys. It would be mean to take away their pleasure.

"Oh, yeah. And look at my hat!" Paul exclaimed,

using the packages he carried to point to the hat on his head. "When we visit the ranch, we need hats, Zach said."

"I'm going to visit the ranch, too," Manuel added in wonder.

"That's wonderful. It will be a great experience for you." Then she looked at Zach and her smile disappeared. "We need to talk."

"Anything wrong? Did the hospital call?"

"No. Nothing. Manuel, your mother is looking for you." She waited as the little boy ran across the landing and opened the apartment door. Then she turned to Paul. "Why don't you take your new things and put them away, sweetie."

"Don't you want to see them first?" the boy asked anxiously, as if he knew she was upset.

"Oh, yes, of course. Come in and show me what you bought." She led the way into the apartment and sat down on the lumpy couch. Five minutes later, Paul had torn open all the packages and had his riches spread around him.

"You made some wonderful selections, Paul. They'll be great for school this year." She was sincere, but she also resented Zach having the pleasure of shopping with her little brother. He'd spent more than she'd planned for Paul, she noticed. And *her* shopping tour wouldn't have been at the expensive stores named on the bags.

"I'll go put them away now," Paul said with a big grin.

She was glad she'd convinced him of her delight. She didn't want him upset.

As soon as Paul left the room, Zach spoke. "Now, tell me the problem. Are you jealous?"

Anger filled her. "Yes! I'm jealous that you spent all and more of the money I'd intended for Paul's clothing. And that I didn't get to...to shop with him."

"I didn't spend your money!" he snapped.

"Yes, you did. How much?"

"None of your business!"

She closed her eyes, then opened them. "Of course it's my business. Why would you spend *your* money on *my* brother. And Manuel. How much?"

Zach stood and began to pace around the small living room. "I'm not going to let you pay for what I purchased. It seemed to me that Paul didn't have much in the way of a wardrobe, so I thought—"

"How generous of you! If you'd told me he embarrassed you, I would've tried harder to find a sitter." Bitterness filled her. This man could afford anything he wanted. He didn't seem to understand how different their lives were.

"Don't you ever say that again! Paul never embarrassed me. He's a wonderful kid."

Her heart swelled with his praise, but his opinion didn't eliminate her difficulties. "Look, I appreciate what you did. You gave both boys a lot of pleasure, but I will, of course, pay for the clothes. Except maybe the cowboy hat and boots."

"You don't like them?"

"They're nice, but not too useful for school wear."

"I wore them to school."

The picture that appeared in her head of Zach as a little boy, clad in his Western wear, was sweet and melted her anger a little, but she didn't agree with him. "You didn't go to school in Kansas City."

"True. But maybe you should consider moving away from here. This isn't a good neighborhood for a little boy to grow up in."

A lot of responses bubbled up in Susan's throat, but she pushed them back. As if she didn't know the dangers inherent in their situation. Hadn't she had nightmares about both Megan and Paul and the possibilities that could occur?

"How much do I owe you?" she asked for the third time.

Before he could answer, there was a knock on the door. Susan swung it open, expecting to see Rosa, and she wasn't disappointed. There was a worried frown on her friend's face.

"Susan, Manuel said— I mean, I'm sorry, but I can't pay—we will pay a monthly amount until—"

Zach stepped forward, interrupting. "Please. The clothes are a gift from me and my grandfather. There is nothing to repay."

"But—but they are so expensive," Rosa protested, wide-eyed, her bottom lip trembling, "and we cannot do anything so grand for our two younger children."

"Rosa," Susan said, taking her friend's hands, "it's okay. Just think of the clothes as an early Christmas present."

"But it's August!"

Susan smiled, letting her sense of the ridiculous take over. "Just tell the children that some Santas have to deliver early because they have so many stops to make."

After that, Rosa expressed her thanks numerous times before she withdrew to her own apartment.

"Damn, I have never had such a hard time delivering a present," Zach protested. Before she could say anything, he felt inside his jacket pocket and drew out a long, thin box. "We'd better get this over and done with, too. You have to wear this because Gramp will expect it."

"Wear what?" she said, staring suspiciously at the box.

He grabbed her left hand. "Where's your wedding ring?"

"In—in my purse. I put it there this morning because I didn't expect to announce... Anyway, that's where it is."

"I need to get it sized, but I'll do that tomorrow. And put this on." He thrust the box at her.

It seemed to Susan that if she opened the box, she would be even more deeply involved in their lie. Zach's unwavering stare, however, made escape impossible. She took the lid off the cardboard box only to discover an elegant box inside. When she opened it, the gleaming diamonds of a tennis bracelet sparkled.

She immediately shut the lid and thrust it back at Zach. "No, I can't accept this."

"Susan, Gramp will have expected me to give you

a wedding present. If I don't, he'll know we're not serious about the marriage." He handed it to her again.

"So—so this is a prop? And when it's over I give it back to you?"

His gaze shifted away from her. "Sure. That's fine. But you need to wear it to the hospital tonight."

"Okay, you keep it until we get to the hospital. I'll put it on then."

"Don't you want to wear it to your sister's tonight?"

"No! They know the marriage isn't real. It would look bad for me to be wearing diamonds that—no. I don't want to wear the bracelet until I have to."

Zach went back to the hotel to shower and change for their evening, irritation filling him. He'd given women diamonds before, in particular, his wife. Every time, the women had shown a lot of enthusiasm…and gratitude…for his gift.

They'd never been shoved back at him.

And the commotion he'd created because he'd bought a few articles of clothing for the boys was absurd. He'd understood a little better Susan's reaction, however, as he'd listened to Rosa. And felt a little less justified. Rosa had told him she had two other children, smaller than Manuel, who had received nothing. That bothered Zach. But he couldn't offer money to Rosa. That would be crass.

Susan and her family and friends were definitely

new experiences for him. But it was because of her that he was in this situation.

When he arrived back at the apartment, Paul and Susan were ready. Paul was wearing one of his new shirts, jeans and cowboy boots. Susan had changed into the powder blue knit outfit she'd worn the first day he'd met her.

She looked beautiful, as always.

The tennis bracelet and wedding ring would add a touch of sparkle, but, of course, she was wearing neither. Irritation filled him.

"Can't you at least wear your wedding ring to your sister's?" he asked as he started the car.

She hesitated, than opened her purse and took out the ring, putting it on her finger. "I'm afraid it might slide off."

Paul spoke from the back seat. "Will Ginny and James be there tonight, too, Susan?"

"More family?" Zach demanded, irritated all over again that these people insisted on meeting him. As if the wedding were real.

"Yes, Paul. Those are the names of Maggie and Josh's children," Susan added for Zach's benefit. "Nate is Kate and Will's little boy."

The short drive was silent after that exchange. Until they pulled into Kate and Will's driveway.

"Nice place. What does the man do for a living?"

"He owns Hardison Enterprises. And Josh has his own security firm. They live near here."

Zach bit his tongue, but he wanted to know why

Susan was living in such a poor section of town when her relatives were obviously loaded.

After they'd entered the house and introductions were made all around, Susan joined the other women in the kitchen, Paul went upstairs to play with his cousins and Zach found himself sitting in the den with the two husbands.

After generalities were exchanged, he asked the question that had been bothering him. "I hope you'll excuse the impertinence of the question, but if you two are doing so well, why is Susan living in that apartment? Don't you know that's not a safe neighborhood?"

He wasn't sure what reaction he'd expected, though both men had seemed decent enough, but laughter wasn't it.

Will Hardison turned to his brother-in-law, Josh, as he chuckled. "It's clear he doesn't know Susan very well."

Josh agreed. "You're right. If he did, he wouldn't ask that question."

"Why wouldn't I?"

"Before either of us knew the girls, Kate and Maggie tried to share what they had with Susan. She wouldn't take anything from them."

"Since then," Josh continued, "we've all tried to help out Susan, but she's too stubborn and proud. We thought we would be able to pay for Megan's room and board and had plans to tackle Susan about it this week. Now we can't even do that."

"We've even offered her a place to live. She won't

accept." Will shook his head. "All three of Mike O'Connor's girls are hardheaded."

"Why did they just get together eighteen months ago? Susan's tight-lipped about her past."

"Her mother left Mike after about six months. She was one mixed-up lady," Josh explained. "Never told him about Susan."

"Then—then Mike isn't Megan and Paul's father?"

"Nope. And we don't know who their fathers were."

"Fathers?"

"Megan and Paul don't have the same father. Susan knows that for sure, but that's about all she knows. I only found out because I was doing the investigation. Susan doesn't volunteer much about her life. But I gather it's been a tough one."

Zach frowned. He kept finding much to admire about Susan.

"If you can find a way to get her out of that hellhole she calls home, we'll be glad to finance it," Will added, watching Zach.

He squared his shoulders. "I don't need financial help to take care of Susan. But, like you, I've not been offered much of a chance."

The other two men nodded solemnly, in complete understanding, which soothed Zach. It was nice to know he had some fellow sufferers.

Susan was surprised at how quickly the three men seemed to have established a friendship. The six adults dined in perfect harmony. The children were fed upstairs by the full-time nanny that Kate and Will employed.

"Your ring is beautiful, by the way," Kate offered during a lull in the conversation.

Susan blushed, automatically hiding her hand in her lap. "Thank you."

"Don't you like it?" Maggie asked.

"Of course I do. It's just that…that since the marriage isn't real—"

"The ceremony was fake?" Will asked, his brows rising.

"No!" Zach returned emphatically. "The ceremony was legal, performed by our minister." Then he shrugged. "What's more, Susan signed a prenuptial agreement that defined the terms of the marriage."

Will chuckled, and Susan and Zach stared at him.

"Sorry. It's just that Kate and I had an agreement, too. And look what happened to us."

"Yeah, I know what you mean," Josh agreed. Susan was embarrassed at the warm look he shot his wife.

"What lawyer did you use, Susan?" Kate asked.

"Lawyer? I didn't use a lawyer," she assured her sister. She didn't understand why Kate even asked that question.

"Oh, my, you should've had representation. Didn't you know that, Zach?" Kate asked.

He shrugged his shoulders, but Susan noticed the frown on his forehead. "There wasn't time."

"Then the agreement probably is worthless," Will assured him. "At least that's what my lawyer said."

Zach stared at Susan. Then he turned back to Will. "I don't think Susan will break our agreement."

"Ah. Well, it's good that you trust each other," Will said with a smile. Kate opened her mouth, as if to argue, but Will shook his head at her and introduced a new topic.

After dinner, Susan and Zach went upstairs and told Paul goodbye, then rushed off to the hospital. They had special visitation privileges, but Gramp would tire if they were too late.

"Zach," Susan said after several minutes of silence, "I want you to know that I'll honor the agreement. If you want me to sign another one, to make it legal, I will, of course."

Zach shot a quick glance at her before turning back to the road in front of him. "I doubt that will be necessary. I know you won't do anything to hurt Gramp."

"No, of course not. How was he doing today?"

"Much better."

Susan noted another frown. "Is something wrong?"

"No. By the way, I like your family."

"Yes, they're nice, aren't they?"

"Why won't you let them help you?"

"Help me? They help me all the time."

"I mean, move you out of that apartment."

Susan bit her bottom lip. Finally, she said, "I'm responsible for Megan and Paul and myself. Not them. My mother was—was irresponsible, but I'm not." She clenched her jaw to keep from saying any more.

"I understand Megan and Paul had different fathers."

"My, you certainly learned a lot tonight. I didn't know Will and Josh were going to spill every family secret." And she'd have a word with them before they got within a mile of Zach again.

"It just came out in casual conversation. After all, you haven't been a fount of information."

"I never realized my personal life was part of the agreement. I agreed to be your temporary fiancée. I did not agree to your becoming my father confessor." Her words came out much sharper than she'd intended. But she wasn't happy with the events of the evening.

"You're not going to make it sound like we're fighting when you talk to Gramp, are you? Otherwise, all our efforts will be worthless."

"Of course not," she said, letting out a deep sigh. The thought of upsetting the old man wasn't acceptable.

Half an hour later, she kept her promise. Sitting on the side of Gramp's bed, she showed him the tennis bracelet and threw loving looks over her shoulder at the handsome man standing behind her.

"Not only did Zach buy me this incredible present, but he took Paul and his friend Manuel shopping. You should see Paul in his cowboy hat. He's so proud!"

"Good. It sounds to me like you and your brother

could use a little pampering,'' Pete returned, smiling as he held her hand.

"No, Gramp, I think this is more spoiling than pampering. I'm going to have to insist that Zach not waste any more money on us." She smiled broadly, hoping to establish some boundaries with a witness.

Neither man responded well to that statement. Zach protested at once. "I think I should spend money on my new family whenever I feel like it."

"Well, of course you should, boy. That's what a husband is for, little lady. To take care of you, provide for you."

In spite of her good intentions, Susan couldn't accept such generosity. "But Paul and Megan are my responsibility, Gramp, not Zach's."

Zach squeezed her shoulder. "We'll discuss this later, honey. We don't want to involve Gramp in our little disagreements."

His warning was clear. "Of course not. Though our spats are few and far between, aren't they, sweetie?" She allowed just the slightest tinge of sarcasm in that last word.

"When are you two going to move out to the ranch? That boy needs to be wearing his boots right now."

Susan almost choked. Moving to the ranch wasn't part of their agreement, was it?

Zach answered before she could. "We're going to wait until you're better. It's easier to visit from here."

"But how's the ranch doing without either of us there?"

"Gramp, you know the guys. They're doing their jobs. I check in by phone every day. Jesse keeps me informed."

Zach's hands still rested on her shoulders, and Susan sat quietly while the two men discussed the ranch. But the skin under Zach's hands was tingling with sensation.

"Well, I think you should all go on back to the ranch. You'll need to get Paul registered in school. I talked to Hester by phone, and she's been getting a room ready for the boy. The one you used as a child, Zach."

"That will be perfect for Paul. Though I'm not sure how he'll manage without his friend Manuel. They're great pals."

"He can have him out for the weekends," Pete suggested. "After all, we want Paul to be happy. You've done a good job raising him, Susan."

"Thank you, Gramp. Um, has the doctor been to see you today?"

"Huh! Yeah, too many times. They ran a lot of new tests today. I told him I didn't need 'em, but he ignored me."

"Why did they do the tests? Did you have any more pain?" Zach asked, leaning toward his grandfather. Which caused his body to press against Susan's back.

She swallowed, unable to concentrate at such close quarters with Zach. She was grateful Zach was questioning Pete about his treatment. Yet she found his body heat strangely comforting...and at the same time, disturbing.

"Naw. No more pain. I'm feeling good."

Zach relaxed, leaning back, removing his body from Susan's, and she breathed a little more easily despite a simultaneous sense of disappointment.

"Good. I thought you were doing better."

As if he'd heard them, the door opened and the doctor appeared. "Good evening, Pete, Mr. and Mrs. Lowery. How is everyone?"

"Fine, Doc. How's Gramp?" Zach asked.

"I'm pleased to tell you he's improved greatly. In fact, he's so much better, we now think we can operate on him and ensure several more years of good health." The doctor beamed at all of them. "He's improved so much that, with your permission, we'll do surgery in the morning, and he'll be able to go home in two days, if all goes well."

"Hot damn!" Pete exclaimed, a smile on his face. "Pack your bags, Susan. We're *all* going home!"

Chapter Seven

After they left Pete Lowery's room, Zach and Susan walked hand in hand down the hallway. He could feel her fingers trembling in his. He figured it was from shock.

Zach could understand why Susan was in shock. He'd led her to believe, hell, he'd believed, that Gramp only had a couple of days to live. Now he was doing so well the doctor could operate, clean out his arteries and talk of several more years of good health, at least.

He opened the car door for her when they reached it. Once he slid behind the wheel, she didn't waste any time asking the question he expected.

"What are we going to do?"

He considered his words. After all, he didn't have any right asking Susan to completely change her life.

But for Gramp's sake, he had to. "Would it be such a hardship, living on the ranch?"

Her hands were tightly clasped in her lap. She kept her face turned away from him. "You mean it? You expect me to uproot Paul and move to your home?"

"Hell, Susan, I know it's a lot to ask. But what can I do? I'm not saying stay forever, but at least until he's recovered from the operation." He held his breath as she considered his words.

She sighed. "What a mess."

"Yeah. But it could be good for you financially. If you and Paul stay until school's out next May, that would give you at least nine months without any rent, food bills, utilities. You could save all that money."

"Yes, but—but how do I explain to Paul? Enjoy yourself but we'll be leaving at the end of the school year? Be careful about making friends, because you'll be leaving them soon?"

"He'll survive. Lots of kids get transferred every year."

"Thanks for caring," she flung back, sarcasm heavy in her voice.

"Paul having to leave his friends doesn't quite rank up there with Gramp's death." He hated to sound brutal, but he was only speaking the truth. Besides, he would do everything he could to make it easier on Paul.

She bowed her head, but she stopped arguing with him. As he pulled into Kate and Will's driveway, she said, "Please don't say anything to Paul yet. I haven't decided."

He sat in the car, waiting for her to return with Paul, wondering what he would do if she didn't agree. Gramp would be devastated. Strangely enough, he realized he, too, would be affected by parting from Susan and Paul. He hadn't planned on that.

Susan returned, holding a sleepy Paul's hand. She helped him into the back seat.

"Tired, buddy?" Zach asked as the little boy greeted him.

"Yeah. I fell asleep."

"Sorry we were so late. Gramp said to give you his love."

"Is he feeling better?"

Zach exchanged a rueful smile with Susan. "Uh, yeah, he's feeling better. He may get to go home in a couple of days."

"Will you go with him?"

"Yeah."

"Oh. I'll miss you."

The sadness in the little boy's voice touched him. "Hey, buddy, we'll still see each other."

"We'll talk about it later," Susan said. "You close your eyes, or you'll be too tired to play with Manuel tomorrow." Then she glared at Zach.

Susan felt boxed in. She wanted to do the right thing for both Paul and Pete Lowery. But she didn't see how she could meet both their needs.

As they climbed the stairs to their apartment, Zach right behind her, she continued to struggle with her decision.

When they reached the top step, she heard Rosa wailing. Pushing Paul toward Zach, along with her keys, she said, "Take him into the apartment. I have to see what's wrong with Rosa."

"Maybe Manny is sick?" Paul suggested anxiously as she knocked on the door.

Rosa, her eyes red, her cheeks tear-streaked, opened the door.

"Rosa, what's wrong?"

"Pedro lost his job," she said with a sob. "They're going out of business. They're not even going to pay him for this week's work. He looked all afternoon for more work, but there was nothing. Oh, Susan, I don't think the landlord will let us stay here."

"Oh, no!" Susan exclaimed, hugging her friend. "Look, I have a little extra money this month—"

"No! We can't take your money. We will—will find something. If not, we'll move in with my mother-in-law." Tears began to roll down her cheeks even as she said the words.

Susan knew how difficult life would be for Rosa in those circumstances, but she couldn't think of anything to say.

"What kind of work does your husband do?"

That quiet question from Zach surprised both of them. Susan let Rosa answer.

"He's a carpenter. And with winter coming—" Rosa stopped and buried her face in her apron.

"A carpenter? Is he home?"

"Yes," Rosa said, "but he's upset. I don't think—"

"I may have a job for him," Zach said calmly, as if he wasn't offering something monumental.

Rosa and Susan stared at Zach and then at each other. Then Susan urged, "Get Pedro."

As soon as Rosa disappeared, she turned back to Zach. "Pedro is a good worker. It would be wonderful if you have something for him."

"We'll see. It depends on his experience."

Before she could question him, Rosa reappeared with Pedro at her side. He looked discouraged.

"Pedro? I'm Zach Lowery," Zach said, extending his hand. "Why don't we go downstairs and discuss a job I have available that you might be interested in."

Pedro silently followed Zach down the stairs. Rosa grabbed Susan's hand and squeezed. "Oh, Susan, if only... Do you think he might hire him?"

"I don't know, Rosa. We'll have to wait and see." She turned to Paul, still standing by their front door. "I've got to get Paul to bed. Is Manuel already asleep?"

"Yes. We tried not to let him know how bad things were, but he could tell something was wrong and was upset." Rosa wrung her hands. "I'm so afraid to hope."

"I'll put Paul to bed, then come back out. Hang on for a few minutes more."

She took her little brother inside and helped him get ready for bed, telling him not to worry. Then she tucked him in with one of his new books and closed the door behind her. She went back outside and settled on the top step with Rosa, putting her arm around her.

The two of them sat silently. There wasn't anything to say. Both knew how important the conference going on down below was to Rosa's future.

When the two men came into view, Rosa squeezed Susan's hand so tightly, she thought it might fall off. Then Rosa sobbed as she stared at her husband. Susan, too, noted the change in his demeanor. His head was up, his shoulders squared. There was hope.

"Rosa, Mr. Lowery has offered me a job. But it would mean moving to his ranch. He said we could have a house—" Pedro said the word reverently "—I would be in charge of building corrals and sheds and general repairs. Mr. Lowery would provide all the tools and he'll pay five hundred a week and all the beef we want to eat."

Susan knew that amount was almost double Pedro's last salary.

Rosa gasped. "H-how much for the house?" she whispered. She had shared her hope for a house with Susan many times.

Zach smiled. "The house comes with the job. It's part of the salary. But I was afraid you might have an objection to living out in the country. The shopping there isn't so great."

"W-we don't have a car. Is there a bus I can take to the store?" Rosa asked. Susan could hear the burgeoning hope in her voice.

"No, but Pedro can drive you into town every once in a while, or you can catch a ride with Hester. In fact, if you can drive, you could take Hester. Her eyesight's not what it used to be. If you want to work, too, Hester could use a little help in the house.''

"Oh!" Rosa dragged out her sigh, unable to believe their good fortune. "Yes, that would be wonderful. Thank you so much. I can't tell you—"

"You and Pedro will be doing me a favor. I'm going to need more help around the ranch now that Gramp needs to slow down. And Hester is over sixty. You're going to find a lot to do."

Pedro grabbed his hand to shake it again. "When shall we start?" he asked anxiously.

"How long will it take you to get ready to move?"

"Our rent is paid through Friday," Rosa said, which was only two days away.

"I can have a couple of hands bring some trucks and help you move on Friday, if that's okay?" As he spoke, Zach reached inside his coat pocket and drew out a checkbook. "I'll pay for the move. Here's a week's salary to take care of whatever else you may need to get ready to move."

Both Rosa and Pedro expressed their thanks over and over again.

"Maybe you'd better wait until you see the house, Rosa," Zach said with a rueful smile. "It's only three bedrooms."

"Three? Three! That's wonderful."

Zach took Susan's hand and backed toward her apartment. "I'm glad you're happy. I'll let you know what time the guys will be here Friday."

"Good night, Pedro, Rosa," Susan said, correctly

interpreting Zach's body language. "I'll send Paul over in the—" Suddenly Susan discovered the downside to Rosa and Pedro's good news. Her childcare had disappeared. What was she going to do with Paul?

"Oh, Susan! I hadn't realized!" Rosa wailed.

"What's wrong now?" Zach asked.

"Who will take care of little Paul? I won't be here," Rosa explained.

"Don't worry," Susan said, forcing a smile. "I'll find someone. Everything will be fine."

Zach reached behind her and opened the door to her apartment. "I may have a solution to that problem, too, Rosa. Don't worry."

Once they were inside the apartment, Susan pulled her hand free from Zach's and crossed her arms over her chest. Rosa had been taking care of Paul, and keeping an eye on Megan after school, too, at one time, since they'd moved there four years ago.

"I do have a solution," Zach said quietly. "One that would thrill Paul."

"Moving to the ranch?"

He nodded. "He and Manuel would still live close to each other. Rosa can keep an eye on him, along with Hester. The only one to suffer would be you because you'd have to drive fifty miles to work each day…if you want to keep working."

"Of course I'd keep working!" she exclaimed. "I wouldn't be able to save any money if I wasn't working."

"As my wife, you'd receive a…an allowance."

Her chin came up. "No, I wouldn't."

He didn't argue, but he stared back at her. "So, are you coming to the ranch?"

She turned her back. "I don't know. Can I at least have until tomorrow morning to decide?"

His hands settled on her shoulders and he turned her around. "Yeah. Will you come with me in the morning for Gramp's surgery?"

"Yes. I told Kate I would be late in the morning. I need to tell Rosa I'll have to bring Paul over early." Her neighbor's name reminded her of Zach's generosity, and a flood of gratitude coursed through her. "Oh, Zach, whatever I decide, thanks so much for what you did for Pedro and Rosa. That was wonderful!"

"Even if it robbed you of a sitter?"

She felt like she'd been slapped. "You think I would stand in the way of an opportunity for them so I could keep Rosa as a sitter?"

His hands left her shoulders and slid down her arms leaving a pleasant tingling sensation in their wake. "Hey, I was only teasing. I may not know you well, but I do know your character better than that."

Mollified, she relaxed a little, only to tense again as he slid his arms around her.

"Shh," he said, smiling down at her. "I just wanted to say thank you for tonight. I know it was hard not to say anything when Gramp talked about all of us moving back to the ranch. You've been terrific through everything."

His rock-hard body was too tempting. Susan

couldn't prevent herself from laying her head on his chest, resting against his strength. "I'm trying to do the right thing, Zach," she whispered. "Only it's hard to know what the right thing *is* here."

His embrace tightened and he nuzzled her forehead. "I think Paul would benefit from some male companionship. It's hard on boys to be around women exclusively."

She jerked up her head. "I do the best I can!"

"Hey, I'm not criticizing you," he said. Then, as if realizing a temptation too sweet to resist, he covered her lips with his.

Susan had both dreaded and longed for this moment. Too many times she'd thought of the feelings that filled her when Zach Lowery touched her. Those kisses they'd shared had stunned her with their intensity, their electricity.

And it was happening again.

She slid her arms around his neck and pressed her body against his. In his arms, she felt more excitement than she'd ever experienced. Yet she also felt safe, secure…whole, something she'd never felt before.

Which was even more frightening.

Was this the way her mother had felt, each time she'd given herself to some man? Wanting a better life than her mother's, Susan had decided long ago she would not seek completion with a man. She would be independent, strong.

She feared Zach made her weak.

Wrenching herself from his arms, she drew deep breaths as she stared out the window of her apartment.

If she'd thought Zach would touch her again—or protest her withdrawal—she was wrong.

"I'll need to pick you up at five-forty-five in the morning," he said matter-of-factly, though his voice was somewhat huskier than usual. "I know it's early, but they'll take Gramp to surgery at six-thirty and I want to see him before they put him under the anesthetic."

Susan turned around, staring at him. He sounded so composed. Had the kiss meant nothing to him?

Apparently not. His expression was grim, but then he was talking about a heart operation for his grandfather.

"No, that will be fine. I'll be ready."

"Then I'd better get out of here so you can get some rest." Without another word, he strode from the apartment, pulling the door closed behind him.

Susan remained standing where he'd left her.

The apartment door opened again.

"Come lock the door, Susan."

Like a zombie, she crossed the room. He bent down, brushed her lips oh-so-gently with his, then pulled the door closed again. "Lock it," he called.

She shoved the dead bolt Josh had installed and leaned against the door. She hadn't wanted Zach to leave. She hadn't wanted him to stop kissing her. She hadn't wanted to be alone.

But she had to be alone. Because her relationship with Zach already had an ending scheduled for next May.

She was *not* going to be her mother all over again.

* * *

Pete Lowery came through the operation like a man half his age. The doctor told Zach his grandfather would be ready to go home Saturday morning, if everything continued to go well.

After the doctor left the room, Zach hugged Susan, hiding his face in her silky hair. Her warmth eased the chill he'd felt inside him ever since they'd carted Gramp away.

And also reminded him of last night.

If she hadn't pulled away, he would've made a colossal mistake the night before. He would've taken her to bed, made love to her until daylight. Because he wouldn't have been able to help himself.

"Thanks for waiting with me," he whispered in her ear.

She pulled back, reluctantly, he thought. "As soon as we see him, I'll need to leave to go to work. He'll understand, won't he?"

"Sure. What about Paul? Did you talk to him this morning?"

"No. I carried him across to Rosa's wrapped in a blanket, still in his pajamas. I hope he went back to sleep."

"When he hears Manny is moving to the ranch, Paul is going to be upset," he reminded her. He couldn't help pushing her to agree to his request that she and Paul move to the ranch with him.

"I know. I—I thought I'd talk to him when I went to the apartment to pick up my car."

"You've made up your mind?" He almost stopped

breathing. As if her decision would determine his happiness. What a ridiculous idea, he told himself. It was for Gramp that he wanted Susan to come. For Gramp.

"Yes. I guess I have no choice. Now not only is it good for Gramp, but it will also be good for Paul."

A disturbing thought occurred to him. "Susan, I swear I didn't offer Pedro the job to force you to come to the ranch."

"I know."

A look passed between them that told Zach she trusted him—that far, at least. He couldn't stop the sense of elation that began deep inside him and flooded his veins, making him momentarily light-headed.

A nurse came into the room. "Mr. Lowery? Your grandfather is in Recovery and awakening, if you and your wife would like to visit with him."

They arrived back at Susan's apartment a little after ten. Anxious about Paul, she hurried up the stairs, Zach right behind her.

When the two boys opened the door to her call, she knew Paul was distraught. As soon as he saw her, he threw his arms around her waist, burying his face against her.

"Paul? Are you all right?"

"Manny's moving away. To the ranch," he sobbed against her.

Manuel stood staring at his friend, torn between the

thrill of moving with his family to a neat place, and the agony of leaving his best friend behind.

"I think that's a good thing," Susan said, glad she'd made her decision.

Paul looked at her in shock. "You do?"

"Well, of course. You'll have a good friend in school with you."

"No, Susan, you don't understand. Manny won't be here. He'll be on the ranch. *Gramp's ranch.*"

"So will you, Paul," she assured him soothingly, a smile on her face.

Paul stared first at her and then at Zach. "I'm going to live with Manny?" he asked, his voice quavering.

"And me and Zach and Gramp. We're all going to live on the ranch this year."

It was almost more than Paul could comprehend. But as he and Manuel figured out the most important thing, that they wouldn't be separated, and the second most important thing, that they'd be on a genuine, honest-to-Pete ranch, they fell into each other's arms with shrieks of excitement.

Rosa came running. "What is it? What's wrong?"

"Oh, Mama, Susan and Paul are coming to the ranch, too!" Manuel told his mother.

Rosa asked a lot of questions, but her excitement, already at a fever pitch, kept up with the boys'.

Susan smiled and answered all the questions, but inside she was frightened at the new direction her life was suddenly taking.

"You will drive into the city every day?" Rosa asked.

As Susan nodded, Rosa asked another question. "Will your car hold up for that kind of drive?"

Susan caught Zach's frown out of the corner of her eye, but she pasted a cheerful smile on her face. "I'm sure it will."

"What kind of car do you have?" Zach asked.

"A compact." Then she changed the subject. "Don't you need to get back to the hospital, Zach? I'll be fine now. Give Gramp our love."

"I will. But right now I want to see your car."

"Why?"

He ignored her. "Paul, you want to come downstairs and point your sister's car out to me?"

Delirious with happiness, the boy never hesitated. "Sure. Come on, Manny. Last one down's a rotten egg!"

"That's dirty pool, Zach Lowery!" Susan protested.

But he didn't wait. With a sly wink at Susan, he followed the boys out of Rosa's apartment.

Chapter Eight

Zach stared at the wreck of a car Paul was pointing to. It was practically an antique, an antique that had been badly mistreated.

He heard Susan behind him and turned around. "Do you ice-skate on those bald tires when it freezes over?"

"I'm going to get new tires with some of the money you gave me," she said hurriedly, her chin coming up.

"New tires won't solve all your problems," he pointed out.

"True. I'll still have to put up with you."

"Don't sass me, lady."

"Don't interfere with my business," she returned.

"What's the matter?" Paul asked, a worried look on his face.

Zach grinned as he watched Susan realize that

she'd have to change her tune so as not to upset her beloved brother. She immediately assured Paul all was well.

"Or it will be when you get a new car." Zach wasn't going to back down on this decision. It would be criminal to let Susan drive fifty miles each way all winter in this jalopy.

"I can't afford a new car." She stepped behind Paul, putting her arms around his neck, and spoke to him, ignoring Zach. "How would you and Manuel like to go to the diner for lunch? Then I could bring you back before I start working."

"Hey, neat! Let's go ask your mom," Paul said to his friend, and the two boys raced up the stairs again.

"I don't know where they get their energy," Zach muttered, watching them until they disappeared from view.

"Look, Zach, I don't want Paul upset, so stop arguing with me in front of him," Susan ordered sternly.

He stared at her, then removed his hat and bent over to brush his lips across hers. As his lips returned to taste more deeply, his arms pulled her against him. The feel of her down his length was as stunning as always.

"Oooh, that's *gross!*" Paul called from the landing.

Zach lifted his head, glad something had distracted him before he completely lost control. "I'll remind you of that remark in a few years, buddy," he called with a grin.

He settled his hat in place, grabbed one more quick kiss and turned to his rental car. "I'll pick you up at the regular time," he called to Susan over his shoulder.

He didn't wait for an answer. In the first place, he didn't want to hear any excuses why she couldn't go with him this evening. And he certainly didn't want their argument to start again.

He'd already made up his mind.

Lunch with the boys didn't involve conversation. All Susan had to do was listen to the excited chatter and speculation about life on a ranch.

"Do you think we'll get to ride horses?" Paul asked, his eyes widening at the sudden thought.

"I don't know, sweetie. You're both a little young."

"We're big enough," Paul asserted, with Manuel nodding.

"We'll see."

After she took the boys back to Rosa, along with lunch for her and her other two children, Susan tried to concentrate on her work. But thoughts about the changes in her life, including Zach's kisses, distracted her.

"Do you need us to keep Paul again this evening?" Kate asked as she popped into Susan's office.

"Oh, thanks, Kate, but he'll stay with Rosa." Susan smiled but ducked her head. She didn't want to tell Kate she was moving to the ranch, though of course she'd have to eventually. Just not today.

"How's Zach's grandfather?"

"He came through the operation well. The doctors are optimistic."

Kate didn't respond and Susan finally looked up.

Then Kate said, "You will let us know if there's anything we can do, won't you, Susan? We're family, remember?"

"I'd never forget that. You and Maggie have made such a difference in my life." This time her smile was sincere, full of warmth.

"Good. Take some time off if you need to."

"Thanks, Kate, but I shouldn't need to. I hope." She suddenly remembered that she'd be moving soon, too. She wasn't sure when, but her rent was due Saturday. She'd have to talk to Zach about that.

Zach hadn't forgotten. When he picked her up that evening, his first question was "Is your rent due Saturday, like Rosa and Pedro's?"

"Yes."

"Then we'll need to move you tomorrow, too."

"I don't think I can get packed, Zach. We're going to the hospital tonight and I work tomorrow."

He crossed his arms over his broad chest and glared at her. "Surely Kate will give you time off."

Of course Kate would. She'd even said as much today. But Susan would need to give the dreaded explanation of her move.

"Well?" Zach prodded when she didn't say anything.

"Yes, of course she will," she admitted with a sigh.

He stepped closer and Susan tensed. She lost all her logic and control when he got close.

"What's the problem, honey?"

"I—I haven't told them I'm moving to the ranch."

"You think they'll be upset with you?"

Frustrated, she glared at him. "*I'm* upset with me. Why wouldn't they be?"

His hands settled on her shoulders and she knew she was in trouble. Backing away, she held up a hand. "Don't—don't come any closer, Zach. We can't—"

To her relief, he stood still. But he continued to stare at her. "Honey, don't get upset. Everything's going to work out just fine."

"That's easy for you to say. I'm the one making all the changes." She was working hard to keep her anger going.

He raised one eyebrow and gave her a rueful smile. "You don't understand men, do you?"

"What do you mean?"

"I'm going to be taking a lot of cold showers with you around. Do you think I'll like that?"

She blushed. And desperately sought to change the subject. "I'd better call Kate before we leave and ask for tomorrow off."

His smile told her he knew what she was doing, but he only nodded in agreement.

She was constantly aware of him as she talked to Kate, grateful he couldn't hear Kate's response when she confessed she was moving to the ranch.

"You're going to what? Are you crazy?"

"I have to, Kate. But it's only temporary."

"That man had better behave himself."

"He will." Lots of cold showers, she reminded herself. She hoped he didn't guess that she'd be needing them, too.

"Wait a minute. I want Will to talk to him. Put him on the phone."

"Kate, no, that's not— Oh, hi, Will. Just a minute."

Zach raised one eyebrow as she held out the receiver to him. "Kate wants to talk to me?"

"No. Kate wants Will to talk to you."

Zach took the phone. "Hi, Will."

"I hear you're taking Susan and Paul to your ranch."

"Yeah. My grandfather had surgery this morning and we're taking him home Saturday."

"I'm glad to hear he's doing well. Is Susan okay with this?"

"She made the decision. I, uh, encouraged her, of course, because I think our breaking up would cause a setback for Gramp, and Paul was pretty enthusiastic. But she agreed."

"Is Susan going to keep working for Kate?"

"Yes. She's planning on driving in every day."

"In that old car of hers? I'll have to insist she let me buy her a better one. It would be dangerous—"

"I've already taken care of it."

"Well, you're two for two. I'm impressed."

"Two for two?"

"You're getting her out of the apartment and giving her a better vehicle. We couldn't convince her on either one of those.''

"So you're not upset with me?" Zach asked, breathing a sigh of relief. Not that their being upset would stop him, because he needed Susan and he believed he was helping her, too. But it would've made things difficult for her.

"Not me. I'm not speaking for my wife, of course." He paused, then said, "Kate says to tell Susan she'll be over in the morning, as soon as she's done a few things at the diner, to help pack up. She'll call Maggie, too."

"I'll tell her. That's nice of them."

"They're family."

Zach hung up the phone after saying goodbye and relayed Will's message.

Tears filled Susan's eyes. "They're so wonderful."

He stepped forward to wrap his arms around her, unable to resist the urge to comfort her, but she backed away again.

"Listen, you're going to have to get used to a little touching, or Gramp will never buy our story," he said. And he'd go crazy if he couldn't touch her.

"It's okay to touch in front of Gramp—or Hester. But not when we're alone." She felt ridiculous making these rules, but she knew they were absolutely necessary.

"Why not?"

"You know why not, Zach Lowery. It's like playing with matches around a gas leak."

He put his hands on his hips and stared at her,

thinking about what she'd said. It was a pretty accurate description of what happened when he touched her. "Okay. I need to talk to Rosa and Pedro. And when we get back from the hospital tonight, I'll start helping you pack. Do you have any boxes?"

"No. I didn't realize— Everything's happening so fast."

He couldn't argue with that statement, either. Last Saturday he only had his grandfather. Now he had a wife—and a lot of other new family when he counted Megan, Paul, Kate and Will with their son, and Maggie and Josh with their two children.

"When am I going to meet Megan?" he asked suddenly.

"I don't know. She doesn't... I haven't talked to her since I met you. She's been so busy trying to find a job and getting used to the campus. I'll have to tell her, but not yet."

"I'm beginning to think you're ashamed of me, Mrs. Lowery," he teased.

"Not ashamed. Just—just finding it difficult to explain what we've done."

"Let's go next door and figure out a schedule. Then we'll go to the hospital. And we don't have to explain anything to anyone." He took her hand before she could move away and pulled her behind him to the front door. At least once they were around people, he could touch her.

She'd agreed to that, whether she realized it or not.

"Pizza's here," Zach called at noon the next day as he came up the stairs.

Susan peeked out her door and saw her handsome husband with pizza boxes stacked to his nose.

"How many did you order?" She would hate to see the bill, but, of course, Zach had already taken care of that. She was discovering he was a very generous man.

"A lot. Cowboys have big appetites. Right, Rick?" One of the cowboys who'd arrived around seven this morning with two trucks and trailers, grinned at Susan. "Yes, ma'am, Mrs. Lowery. We eat a lot."

"Well, you've certainly earned your lunch. Your help has been invaluable." She had a lot of people to thank. Kate and Maggie had arrived around nine this morning and were still packing the few things left in her apartment.

"I'll call the others to lunch," she said.

"After we eat, I think we'll be ready to head for the ranch," Zach said as she turned away. "Don't you think?"

"We're almost finished, yes," she agreed, but she was reluctant. She'd been hanging over the edge of the cliff for four years, just barely making it. Now she felt like she was being asked to let go and trust that someone would catch her. After life with her mother, she wasn't into trusting men all that much.

Zach looked as if he was about to ask a question she didn't want to answer, so she ran for the two bedrooms. "Pizza's here for lunch," she called to her half sisters.

"Pizza?" Kate asked in sudden outrage. "I could've had a real meal sent over from the diner."

"Kate, pizza will do," Susan insisted. "You've already contributed enough, both you and Maggie. You brought over a cooler of drinks, and you've done a lot of packing." And some arguing, too. Kate, in particular, had wanted Susan to think about what she was doing. Maggie had recommended caution, but she was visibly delighted that Susan was leaving her apartment.

"But *we* could've helped her get out of here," Kate had insisted.

"Yes, but you know she's too proud to take our help," Maggie had added.

"No, it's not that, it's just…I can't be your responsibility." Susan had dashed away the tears that filled her eyes. "We're making it, you know. And now I have money to pay for Megan's room and board."

Kate and Maggie exchanged frustrated looks.

Then Maggie said, "Just remember. If things don't work out with—at the ranch, you let us know. We'll call it a loan, if you want, but we'll help you."

"You guys are the best," Susan whispered.

"Hey, I thought *I* was the best guy," Zach had said from behind her. Her sisters laughed, but Susan had to struggle to meet his lighthearted tones.

"Aren't you, though. Well, I have to get to work."

But the time was drawing near for her to turn loose of her hold, to face the changes in her life. All because of a lie that had seemed such a good cause—and so uncomplicated. Hah!

As everyone sat down on boxes, a slice of pizza in

hand and soda nearby, Susan tried to count her blessings. But the change was still distressing.

Zach moved a box with his foot next to the one Susan was on and sat down with his pizza and drink. "I thought the packing would take all day, but thanks to everyone's hard work, we're going to be ready to roll in a few minutes."

"We'll need to write down your telephone number and mailing address, Zach," Maggie said. "Even if Susan comes into town every day, we may need to talk to her at night."

"No problem. We're not keeping her prisoner." Then he leaned over toward Susan and kissed her. The kiss was brief, but her heart rate jumped and she had difficulty facing everyone. He wasn't breaking their agreement, of course, because she'd said they could touch in front of others. Still, she hadn't expected him to be quite so...enthusiastic about it.

"When will your grandfather go home?" Maggie asked.

"In the morning," Zach said with a smile. "I'm going to get my family settled. Then I'll come back with the helicopter and bring him home."

Silence fell, but then Zach reached out and took Susan's hand. "I didn't think I'd be bringing him home alive. But thanks to Susan, we are."

She closed her eyes, trying to hold back tears. Gramp was the reason for their lie. She had to keep that in her mind.

Zach's lips covered hers and her eyes flew open.

Pulling back, she muttered, "Zach, everyone's watching."

"I know," he agreed, grinning. He was reminding her of her promise.

"I think it's time to finish loading." Even moving to the ranch seemed less risky than letting him kiss her.

"We're ready to go, Zach," Rick called. His truck had a small back seat, and Rosa and her two smaller children were already there. Pedro was standing beside Rick, a big smile on his face.

"Susan, can I ride with Manuel?" Paul asked.

"I don't think there's room, Paul. You'd better ride with me. Manuel can come with us if he wants."

"But the truck is lots neater, Susan," Paul pleaded.

"Why don't you let Paul and Manuel ride in the other truck?" Zach suggested. He hoped to send Paul on his way before Zach surprised Susan with his latest purchase. "I need to drop off the rental car. I thought maybe I could ride with you."

She looked at him suspiciously, but he only smiled at her.

"I suppose I could, if Chuck won't mind." She looked at the other cowboy who, after a quick look at Zach, said he'd be delighted to entertain the two eight-year-old boys for an hour.

The boys shouted their happiness and scrambled into the front seat of the second truck.

"We'll be right behind you," Susan shouted, waving as the trucks pulled out.

Kate and Maggie hugged her, asking her to call once she got there.

"It may take a little longer," Zach warned, ignoring Susan, who had turned to stare at him. "I thought we'd drop by the hospital and check on Gramp before we started out. You don't mind, do you, Susan?"

She frowned but shook her head no.

Kate and Maggie got into Maggie's car and left.

Only Zach and Susan remained in the parking lot.

"I told Rosa we'd be right behind them," she said, chewing her bottom lip.

"We'll be there in time for dinner."

"Well, I'll follow you to the car rental." She turned around to go to her car...then came to an abrupt halt. In the place where she thought she'd parked her car was a four-wheel-drive sports utility vehicle. She walked closer to look on the other side, in case she'd parked one space over.

"Zach, my car isn't here."

He stretched out his hand with a set of keys. "Yes, it is. That silver SUV is yours. You'll need it this winter to get to work."

"No," she said, backing away from him.

"Come on, honey, your car isn't here. You have to drive that one."

"Zach, you can't do this. You have no right—"

"To provide for and protect my wife? I beg to differ." He stepped closer to her. "And to thank you for saving my grandfather's life. What value would you put on his life, Susan? Less than that car?"

"Zach! I never... You can't *pay* me for Gramp's recovery."

"You're right. If I gave you everything I have, I couldn't repay you for Gramp's recovery. So let me express my appreciation with a car that you desperately need. You'll have to admit your car wouldn't make it on a cold morning."

"That has nothing to do—"

"So you want me to get out of bed and come after you every time your car breaks down?" He gave a proper hangdog expression. "Of course I'll do that, but I hate to get out of bed on a cold morning. But if you want to torture me..." He tried to look thoroughly miserable. If his wife knew anything about a cowboy's life, she'd throw something at him, but he was betting she didn't.

She frowned at him and drew a deep breath. "I'll use the car until I move back to Kansas City. Then it will be yours."

"Agreed," he said cheerfully. "Now, let me show you a few things about a four-wheel drive. Then we'll be on our way."

He had Susan slide behind the wheel and showed her what she'd need to know to drive it home. "You promise you'll follow me?"

"Of course. Why wouldn't I?"

"I was afraid you'd be mad at me."

"I should be. I think I've been manipulated."

"Naw, honey. That couldn't happen. Start the engine."

She turned the key and the powerful engine roared to life.

"Seat belt," he reminded her, and helped her fasten it.

"Zach, I'm not a child."

"Don't I know it." Then he leaned over and kissed her, relieved to have gotten her to accept the vehicle. And dying to touch her.

She pushed him away. "Zach, there's no one around."

"Not true. I definitely saw one of your neighbors go up the stairs."

"That doesn't count!" she scolded.

"Oh, sorry. My mistake. Let's go home," he said, his voice husky with desire. "I'll have lots of excuses to kiss you there."

Chapter Nine

As she drove the new vehicle toward her new home with her new family, Susan thought she'd faced everything. What else could there be?

She found the answer to her question when she and Zach arrived at the Lowery Ranch. First of all, she was unprepared for the elegance and size of the ranch house. It was big enough to house a huge family.

Hester came to the back door as Zach led her to the porch. "Welcome, Mrs. Lowery," she said, bending her head.

Susan smiled and took her hand. "Please, call me Susan. I'm not quite used to my new last name."

Hester smiled. "Okay. Paul has already moved into his room. He's a fine boy."

"Oh, Hester, thank you so much. I hope he hasn't been any trouble."

"Nope. He and Manuel like my cookies just fine, so I reckon we'll get along."

Zach laughed. "I don't know of any kid who doesn't like your cookies, Hester, and maybe a few big guys, too."

"You always did. Better show the missus to the master bedroom. Pete told me to move him out and you in."

Susan felt Zach tense beside her, and she turned to frown at him. What was wrong?

"I didn't intend to move him out," Zach protested.

"He knows that. But he's thrilled about it. You know he wants you and Susan to be happy here." She turned to precede them into the house. "And I reckon you've got a lot better chance this time."

Susan raised her eyebrows. She had yet to hear anything good about Zach's first wife.

She started to follow Hester into the house and found herself suddenly upended as Zach swung her into his arms. "Lowery tradition," he whispered. "The bride is carried across the threshold."

"But you've already— Oh! Okay, we're in. You can put me down." Her voice was breathless, as if she'd run a race.

He slowly lowered her to her feet but kept his arms wrapped around her. "Welcome home, Mrs. Lowery." Then his lips covered hers.

The problem with the agreement that he could kiss her in front of others was that she forgot anyone else was around, Susan thought ruefully. His touch was overwhelming, lifting her into a fantasyland that began and ended with his arms. He lifted his lips, but then returned them to her mouth before she could regain control of her senses.

"Here now, boy, take that business to your bedroom. You've got an hour before dinner," Hester said with a twinkle in her eye.

Susan, turning a bright red, glanced away from the older woman, afraid she might see the longing Susan was feeling.

Zach gave his housekeeper a lopsided grin. "Good idea, Hester. We'll see you at dinner." He kept his arm around Susan as he led her to the door that gave access to the rest of the house.

As soon as the door swung closed behind them, Susan pulled away from him. "Your house is beautiful...and huge!"

"Yep. You'll have a little more room than in the apartment. Except for one thing."

"One thing? What are you talking about?"

"I'll show you." He led the way up a beautiful curving stairway, then opened the first door on the left. "The master bedroom."

She stepped into a cavernous room appointed with gleaming mahogany furniture. Admiring the rock fireplace and navy flowered sofa in front of it, Susan gasped. "Oh, it's beautiful."

"Yeah." When she turned to look at him, he repeated, "It's the *master* bedroom."

With all the changes in her life, Susan didn't grasp his meaning at once. When she did, her mouth fell open. "You—you mean you'll—"

"Gramp and Hester expect both of us to sleep here."

Susan turned to stare at the king-size bed. "But—but..." She couldn't do this. Not without breaking her promise to herself. Her mother had slept with almost any man who happened to be around, and Susan had promised herself she wouldn't follow that pattern. Her husband would be her first and last lover.

She almost choked when she remembered the man beside her *was* her husband. But he didn't plan on their marriage lasting.

"Don't worry. I'm going to keep my promise."

"How?" Her stark question didn't offer compromises.

"Not interested in changing the rules?" he asked, still grinning, but Susan recognized the seriousness in his question.

"No."

He sighed. "I was afraid of that. I've got an air mattress and pump in that package I put in your car. I'll sleep in the dressing room."

After holding herself so tensely, Susan began to tremble as she realized Zach intended to keep his word. It would've been so easy for him to persuade her, to take her without asking. But he hadn't.

"Th-thank you, Zach," she whispered.

He wrapped his arms around her. "I'm not breaking our agreement. I'm supporting your shaky knees, not seducing you."

Whatever he called it, she found his warmth comforting. Indeed, she couldn't remember ever experiencing the like before. She hoped it wouldn't become addictive, but feared it already had.

Zach settled down on the air mattress later that night. Susan had covered it with sheets and a blanket or two. Her perfume hung in the air, teasing his senses.

He was in a bind.

When he'd offered Susan money to play his fiancée, he'd assumed their association would be short-lived. Now he was bringing Gramp home tomorrow, and he and Susan were married.

His view of Susan had changed a lot in the last few days. Her beauty remained constant, of course. But he was also discovering in her an inner beauty that had such depth, such richness, that he was stunned.

Not raised around any woman but Hester, he hadn't been prepared for his first wife's greed and selfishness. He'd gone into shock shortly after the marriage, then gritted his teeth and tried to survive.

And hadn't done a very good job.

He'd told himself marriage would never be an option for him again. After all, he couldn't hide who he was. Or his wealth. But with Susan, he had to work hard to give her anything. She was so stubborn and independent, so selfless, that he had difficulty believing she was real.

Except when he held her.

He twisted to his side, hoping to dismiss such thoughts. If he couldn't, he wouldn't get much sleep tonight.

* * *

Pete Lowery returned to the ranch Saturday afternoon. He moved into the downstairs bedroom next to Hester's, so she could take care of him.

But with the door open, his bedroom became the family room. Paul and Manuel visited him frequently, asking endless questions about the ranch, until Susan chased them out.

But Pete loved having the two boys around. He encouraged both of them to call him Gramp. And both boys were thriving.

On Monday, Susan's first day back at work, she dressed in the powder blue knit, one of her favorite outfits, and hurried down the stairs to the breakfast that Hester had insisted on fixing.

Susan had made one change in her plans. She'd decided to take Paul with her each day until school started. After all, he was her responsibility. And she felt she was losing control. For eight hours a day, with Paul beside her, she could pretend nothing had changed.

"'Morning, Hester," she called as she gave the woman a hug.

"'Morning to you, Susan. You are such a ray of sunshine. I love your smile."

"It's easy to smile with all the help you give me. I hope I'm not leaving too early for you. I don't want to lengthen your day."

"Lawsy, child, I've been up since six. Your husband had breakfast at six-thirty. Didn't you notice he was gone?"

Susan flushed bright red. "Uh, yes, of course, but I didn't know when he took breakfast." That sneak, all his talk about having to get up early to help her with her old car.

"'Morning," Zach called from the door, spinning Susan around. He immediately kissed her, making her knees weak.

"I—Hester said you've already had breakfast."

"That I have, and done a little work. But I'm going to have another cup of coffee with you."

She wasn't going to let him think she hadn't figured out his lie. "I thought you slept late."

"I never said that, honey," he told her with a grin.

"You two sit down. Your eggs are ready," Hester ordered, ignoring their conversation.

"Hester, Paul should be down any minute. Then we'll leave for the city as soon as he's eaten."

"When will you take him for registration?" Hester asked.

"I don't know. I'll have to ask Kate about the best day to take off." Susan frowned, worrying about another day off from work.

"Hey, I can take Paul and Manuel to school," Zach offered. "How old is Manuel's sister? Does she need to register, too? I can take Rosa with me."

"Josefina is five. She'll start kindergarten this year," Susan replied. "Are you sure you have time? I don't want to cause a conflict with your work schedule."

"I'm sure."

Paul entered the kitchen, still in his pajamas and rubbing his eyes.

Susan greeted him with a hug. "Why aren't you dressed, sweetie? We'll need to leave in a few minutes."

Zach frowned. "Paul's going with you? Why?"

"Because he's my responsibility," she assured him sharply. Of course, with Rosa at the ranch, she was going to have to make other arrangements for his care until school started, but she'd find a way.

"Don't be ridiculous. Paul, wouldn't you rather stay here on the ranch?" Zach asked.

"Yeah! Me and Manuel can explore and—"

"Paul!" Susan swallowed and tried to calm down. "That's too much work for everyone."

Hester was watching her from the stove, and Paul's big eyes were on her. Zach raised one eyebrow as he, too, stared.

"Susan," he finally said, "Rosa and her three children will be here with Hester. What's one more?"

"Rosa is supposed to help Hester with the house."

"She will. And will probably have more time if Paul is here to play with Manuel. Besides, I have some jobs for the boys. Everyone on a ranch has chores to do."

Paul's excitement about work took Susan aback.

"I don't think—"

"Please, Susan! Please? I'll be very good."

Anger filled her at being put in the position of the bad guy. And she knew where to lay the blame. "Very well."

As soon as she finished her breakfast, without any more conversation on her part though the other three chatted, she rose. "Zach, could you walk me to my car?"

"With all the pleasure in the world, honey," he assured her with a grin.

She'd see if he was still thinking of pleasure when she finished with him.

Zach followed Susan out the door, enjoying the view as her trim hips swung in a mesmerizing rhythm. She seemed upset, but he didn't think it could be anything serious. Things were going too well.

He changed his mind when she swung around to glare at him. "Zach Lowery, *I* am Paul's guardian! Not you. I make decisions about him. Don't put me in the position of being the bad guy again."

He gave a shrug of exasperation. "Honey, it didn't make sense for you to drag the little guy all the way into the city when he could stay here and enjoy himself."

"Then ask me in private," she flung back. "I make the decisions about my family."

He leaned over and kissed her briefly. "Okay. I get the picture. Drive carefully." Then he opened the door to her vehicle, hoping to avoid any further tirades.

"You—you frustrate me so much! Don't be so nice!"

He cupped her cheek. "Honey, you don't know what frustration is until you've tried mine." He kissed her again, and she wrenched away from him and got in, slamming the door.

Standing there, his hands on his hips, he watched her race down the long drive, hoping she calmed down before she reached the main road.

Then he went back in the house to explain to Paul that they were going to have to be careful not to upset Susan. He was beginning to think that might be a lifelong goal for him.

At lunch, Hester took a tray into Pete and then invited Rosa and her children, Zach and Paul to sit down to eat. After everyone had been served, she said, "We had a strange phone call this morning."

"Yeah?" Zach replied, but his thoughts were on Susan.

"Someone asking for Susan Greenwood."

His head snapped up. "Who was it?"

"I don't know. I said she'd married you and her name was Susan Lowery now."

He exchanged a worried look with Rosa. "What did the person say?"

"Well, she sort of gasped and asked me if I was sure. Then she wanted to know how to get here." She took a bite of meat loaf. "I figured it couldn't be some old girlfriend of yours, so I told her."

"Okay, thanks for letting me know, Hester." He turned his attention to his food, but his mind toyed with the identity of the caller.

After lunch, Rosa's little ones had to take a nap,

and Zach was going to show Manuel and Paul the chores he'd lined up for them.

The boys followed him eagerly to the barn. When he told them they'd be paid for their work, they were over the top. "Zach, we'll work for free," Paul said earnestly.

"I know you would, buddy, but on the Lowery Ranch, everyone gets paid for his or her work. And I expect you to do a good job. I'll be inspecting it when you're finished."

After showing them what to do, he went about his business, only dropping a word with a nearby cowboy to check on his new employees occasionally.

His eyes scanned the ranch house, looking to see if there had been any new arrivals, but he couldn't see any strange vehicles. With a shrug, he went about his business.

Four hours later, sweaty and tired, he came back to check out the boys' work. He was pleasantly surprised by their thoroughness.

"Congratulations, boys. You did a great job. We'll go up to the house and you'll get your pay."

Beaming with pride, Paul straightened his shoulders. "Susan said I couldn't take anything else from you 'cause we're already living here free."

"But I'm not offering you a gift, Paul," Zach said seriously, figuring he was going to have to have yet another talk with Susan. "You and Manuel both earned your money. You worked hard."

"Yeah, we did," Manuel agreed.

Paul swallowed. "Okay. I'll go ahead and take the

money, but then I'll have to ask Susan if I can keep it.''

Now Zach knew he had to talk with Susan before Paul did.

"Good idea. Like I said this morning, we don't want to upset Susan."

Both boys nodded. He led the way out of the barn, only to come to an abrupt halt. Across the way, by the corral, he saw several of his cowboys gathered, not working. That in itself was unusual enough, but the blonde in the center of the circle looked remarkably like Susan. She was back home already?

He started toward her, but Paul suddenly gave a yell and outran him. "Megan!"

The lady pushed her way through the admiring cowboys and gave all her attention to her brother. "Paul!" She ran toward him, her arms open wide.

They both hugged and then talked so fast neither could understand the other. Zach decided it was time he introduced himself to the last of Susan's siblings.

"Hi, Megan."

She turned from Paul and stared at him. "Are you Mr. Lowery?"

"It's Zach," Paul said, grinning at the man. "He's neat."

"Thanks, buddy. Yeah, I'm Zach Lowery. Have you been to the house?"

"No. I—I was afraid. I didn't think Susan would be there, and I thought maybe I'd wait until she got back. She will be coming here tonight, won't she?"

"Yeah." He looked at his cowboys. They were still

staring at Susan's little sister, their tongues practically hanging out. "I'll take care of Megan now, guys. You can go back to work."

Reluctantly, they sauntered away after telling her goodbye. Zach laughed. "We're going to have to look for some ugly dust around here, or I won't get any work out of those guys."

"Oh, I'm sorry. I didn't mean—"

He took her arm, turning her toward the house. "I'm kidding, Megan. It's just that between you and Susan, these boys have never seen such beautiful women."

She blushed and grinned at him.

"We'll go to the house and introduce you to Hester and my grandfather. I guess you already know Rosa."

She stopped walking, turning to look at the two boys following them. "It was so natural to see you and Manny together, Paul, I didn't realize he shouldn't be here. How—"

"We live here now," Manuel said proudly. "Me and Paul still get to be together."

Zach offered a more coherent explanation. "Pedro lost his job and I happened to have an opening here. And Rosa is helping Hester, our housekeeper. She's getting on in years but won't consider retiring."

"How wonderful. But when did you and Susan meet, and why didn't she ask me to the wedding?"

"Everything happened pretty fast. I guess you'll have to talk to Susan about that," he said, hoping Megan wouldn't ask any more questions. Though he had one of his own. "How did you know where Susan and Paul were?"

"I got a phone message from Susan giving the number here at the ranch in case I needed her for an emergency. It worried me, so I called it, and someone told me you two were married and how to get here. So I came."

Zach assured her she was welcome.

Inside the house, Megan met Hester and exchanged a hug with Rosa. Then Zach took her into Pete's bedroom.

"Gramp, I'd like you to meet Megan, Susan and Paul's sister. She's come down from the University of Nebraska to find out what her family's up to."

Pete was delighted. In no time, he had Megan sitting on the side of his bed, telling him all about life on campus. After they'd chatted for half an hour, he asked her if she'd consider transferring to Kansas University. After all, she'd be able to come home on weekends if she did.

Zach had no objection to Gramp's suggestion, but after his conversation with Susan that morning, he didn't think she would be happy with it.

"I might. I've been lonesome, missing Susan and Paul."

"How did you get here?" Zach asked. He was sure she didn't have a car at school.

"I caught a ride with a guy driving to Kansas City. He offered to drop me off here."

"A friend?"

"A friend of a friend. You know how it is at college," she said with a shrug.

Another reason to talk to Susan. Zach knew *exactly* how it was at college. Date rape as well as other perils awaited young, naive women.

"That doesn't sound too safe."

"I'm fine," she assured him, but her cheeks flushed.

"I hear a car. That's probably Susan," Zach warned. "You want to face her alone or with all of us around you to protect you?"

"Protect me from Susan? That's ridiculous," Megan exclaimed. After looking at those around her, she asked, "Isn't it?"

Chapter Ten

She'd been a shrew.

All the way home, Susan prepared her apology to Zach.

After all, it wasn't his fault that her brother preferred staying on the ranch and playing with his friend to driving an hour each way with her and being bored to tears. Or that Zach's suggestion made him appear the hero and her the villain.

It wasn't.

She just needed to remind him that discussing suggestions about Paul in front of the boy was not a good idea.

That wasn't being unreasonable.

And that was her goal. Everything had happened very fast, but Zach was keeping his word. He was sleeping on a miserable air mattress while she sprawled out in the luxurious huge bed. He'd been discreet, staying downstairs for half an hour each night so she could have the bathroom to herself before he came up.

He was being a gentleman, and she was going to be a lady.

She parked the SUV where Zach had shown her Friday. When the weather got colder, he'd told her she could use one of the garages, but for now she could park it near the back door.

With a sigh, she got out and headed for the house, anxious to see how Paul had managed.

The kitchen was empty except for Hester, who indicated everyone was in Gramp's room. With a smile, Susan turned left instead of climbing the stairs. She had to check on Paul before she could change her clothes and relax.

The room seemed full. Zach, Paul, Manuel and Gramp were all staring at her, and Megan was—*Megan!*

"Megan!" she exclaimed, rushing to her sister and embracing her while her mind raced with the implications of Megan's appearance. "What are you doing here? Is everything all right?"

"I'm fine, except I'm mad at you for not inviting me to your wedding, even if it was quick!"

Susan glared at Zach over Megan's shoulder, forgetting about the rest of her audience. She stepped back from Megan's embrace and searched her sister's face. "I—I couldn't... Didn't Zach explain?" she asked, hoping to buy some time.

"It was my fault," Pete said, and Susan held her breath for what he would say next.

"I thought I was dying, and I didn't want them to wait to get married. So I begged them to do it at once in my hospital room. I suspect Susan hated to tell you about the wedding because she knew you'd be upset about missing it. The poor thing's been caught between a rock and a hard place."

Susan stared at Gramp, grateful for his summing up of events in a way that might eliminate some questions. But something in his gaze disturbed her.

Megan hugged her again. "Oh, Susan, how horrible for you. And I'm glad it didn't turn out that you were terminally ill, Mr. Lowery," she added, beaming at Pete.

"You and me both. But call me Gramp. We're all family here." His attention switched back to Susan. "I'm trying to talk this little girl into changing schools. She could go to Kansas University and come home on weekends. She's really missing her family."

Susan immediately glared at Zach, but he shook his head no. "I think it's a good idea, honey, but I didn't come up with it and I haven't tried to promote it."

"What? You don't want Megan to be a part of the family?" Pete demanded, outrage in his voice.

"Of course I do. But I think decisions about Megan and Paul's choices should be up to them and Susan."

Susan smiled her apology. "That's very sweet of you, Gramp, but Megan is on scholarship at Nebraska. If she transferred, she might not get any scholarships at KU, and I couldn't afford—"

"Now, girl, you know we have plenty of money," Pete began.

"Megan and I will discuss it," Susan replied hurriedly. "In fact, if you don't mind, I'll take Megan upstairs and have—have a little girl chat." Frantically, she tried to organize her experiences of the past few days to explain the situation to Megan.

"Oh, but—" Megan began.

Zach intervened, which made Susan wonder what was going on. "I think you'd better go have a chat with Mother Hen, here. She gets a little anxious about you two."

Megan laughed. "She is a mother hen, isn't she? But she's the best sister. Even before Mom died, Susan's the one who took care of us, provided for us. And since Mom died, Susan's been our mother and big sister both. She even tried to pay off Mom's debts, which were substantial." She sighed. "Poor Mom was a failure as a mother *and* as a provider."

"Megan! Don't...never mind. Come on." Susan marched out the door, hoping her sister would follow without any more revelations.

"Thanks for making me feel so welcome," Megan said as she followed her sister.

Pete Lowery sent Paul and Manuel to ask Rosa if Manuel could eat with them that evening, telling the boys to help Hester with setting the table when they got back.

Zach waited until the boys were gone, knowing

Pete had sent them away on purpose. His grandfather had something to say.

"Don't you think it's about time you told me the truth about Susan?" Pete growled.

Zach caught his breath, then said, with as much control as he could muster, "What do you mean?"

Pete pushed another pillow behind his head. "You and that little lady have been pitching a lot of lies. If you're not careful, you're going to step in some of them."

"Gramp, we—"

Pete held up his hand. "I believed them at first. And I'm grateful for the effort. Not only that, I think she's the best thing to happen to you in a long time. I'm just afraid you're going to mess things up if you don't straighten out a few things."

Zach gave up. With a long sigh, he pulled up a chair beside Gramp's bed and sat down. "You're okay? This hasn't upset you?"

"Damn right it's upset me. You've got to marry that girl before she gets away."

"We are married," Zach reminded him.

"Yeah, and that's why you look at her like a hungry bear licking his chops, admiring the latest tourist. Boy, I'm not an idiot!"

"Okay, we're technically married, but we're not— I mean, it's in name only."

Pete grunted. "I knew it."

"Hell, Gramp, what was I supposed to do? I'd lied to you about there being a woman in my life. Then, on your deathbed, you asked to see her. I couldn't confess my sins then. It might've sent you over the edge.''

"So how did you meet her?''

"Just like I told you. But it was the day I brought you to the hospital, not before.''

"She agreed, just like that?''

"I paid her." He hated confessing that, because he didn't want Gramp to think any less of Susan, but honesty seemed like a good idea now. In fact, it was a downright relief.

Pete's eyes narrowed. "Has she been gouging you?''

Zach couldn't hold back a chuckle. "No. She wanted to give me back half the money. She didn't want any more to marry me, and she tries to reject everything I give her. The wedding ring, tennis bracelet and car are 'loans,' in her mind.''

"Ah. I thought she was a good girl.''

Zach smiled, a thousand pictures of Susan running through his mind. "Yeah," he said softly.

"You're in love with her.''

Zach jerked as if he were in the electric chair and someone had thrown the switch. "What? No! I—''
He stopped and turned to stare at his grandfather, wonder gathering in his gaze. "Yes," he said slowly. "Yes, you're right. I'm in love with her. I want to care for her, protect her, have her beside me and— and love her till death do us part.''

He'd realized his opinion of Susan had changed. And he'd recognized his physical attraction to her.

But he hadn't figured out what that meant until his grandfather said it. "Dear God, I'm in love with her."

"Praise be," Pete murmured. "I was afraid you'd grown too cynical, boy." He cleared his throat, as if trying to hide some emotion. "Now," he continued briskly, "what are you going to do about it?"

Zach stared at him blankly. "Do?"

"To keep her. You want to keep her, don't you?"

"Of course I do, but… I made her a promise."

"What promise?"

"That I wouldn't take advantage—that she could decide what she wanted from the marriage."

"In other words, no bedding her," Pete said in disgust.

Zach gave his grandfather a half smile. "Not unless she asks me to."

"Hellfire, boy, what kind of damn fool agreement is that?"

"I kind of felt obligated, since I was asking her to marry me the day after I met her. Besides, I didn't know I'd fall in love with her."

"Well, we'll figure out something to make it all come out right. We're not letting Susan get away. She's a Lowery now."

"Right," Zach agreed, but he wasn't sure how he'd convince Susan of that.

"And we have to hurry. I want to start those babies on the way," Pete said, rubbing his hands together.

"Oh, Susan," Megan squealed as she followed her sister up the stairs. "It's a dream come true. Zach is so handsome and nice…and he's rich!''

Susan said nothing.

"You're the luckiest woman in the world. And no one deserves it more!''

No response. Susan opened the door to the master bedroom and Megan exclaimed on its beauty and Susan's good fortune again.

"Megan, stop it!'' Susan finally protested, close to tears.

"But it's all so gorgeous. I could—Susan? Susan, why are you crying?'' Megan asked, running to her sister's side as she slumped down on the bed. "What's wrong?''

"It's not wonderful,'' Susan said, sniffing. "I'm not the luckiest woman in the world.'' She lay across the bed, covering her face with her arms.

"But—but Zach is handsome.''

Susan nodded but kept her face covered.

"And he's rich.''

Susan nodded again.

"And this is a wonderful— Oh, Susan, does he hit you?'' Megan demanded in dramatic tones. "Is that it? I'll take him apart if he dares to—''

"No!'' Susan protested, almost strangling on her tears as she sat up. "No, of course not. He's been…perfect.''

"Then what's the problem? You've landed in paradise!''

Susan wiped away her tears. "Paradise has a revolving door.''

"I don't understand," Megan said, anxiously leaning toward her big sister.

"It's all a pretense. We started out with the best of intentions, but things have gotten out of hand." She explained how she had met Zach and their original agreement, followed by the complication of Gramp's improvement.

To her surprise, Megan burst out laughing.

"I'm glad you think it's so funny!" she snapped.

"I'm sorry, Susan, but you'll have to admit, the way you tell it, that scene must've been—" She stopped as Susan continued to glare at her, and tried to compose herself. "I mean, you can't wish for something bad to happen to Mr. Lowery."

"Of course not! That's why we're in this ridiculous position."

"But it has its good side. I mean, we've got some extra money, and you and Paul get to live here for a school year." Megan looked at her sister, as if trying to see if she'd cheered her up at all.

Susan tried. She moved her lips into what should've been a smile. She nodded her head in agreement. And she didn't convince either herself or her sister.

"I'm—I'm going to be able to save a lot of money, so maybe we can get a better place to live and have money for room and board at college saved up for next year." By the time she finished speaking, tears were running down her cheeks.

"Why are you crying?"

"Because I'm in trouble." For the first time, she

admitted what she'd known for several days. "Do you remember Mom? How her life revolved around whatever man she was with at the time? How she forgot all about us if a man even offered her a compliment?" Susan bowed her head. "How sleeping with some man was more important than anything in the world?"

Megan shrugged her shoulders. "I just knew she wasn't there, didn't care about us. You were the one who reassured us, cared for us, loved us."

"I don't want to be like her!"

Megan stared at her, then burst out laughing. "Oh, Susan, that's a ridiculous thought! You couldn't possibly—"

"Yes, I could. When Zach touches me..." She stared into space, fighting her temptation in her mind.

Megan leaned over and cupped her sister's cheek. "You're in love with him."

"No." She knew she was lying, but it was important that Megan not know just how difficult it was for her. "No, but I'm attracted to him."

"Have you slept with him?"

Susan stared at her, horrified. "No. I won't be like Mom."

"Susan, how many men have come on to you? You're beautiful. I know you attract men the way honey attracts bears."

"What does that have to do with anything?"

"Did you respond to any of the others? Were you tempted to give yourself to them?"

"Of course not!"

"Why is Zach different?"

Susan knew the answer to that question. But there was a time limit on paradise. That's why she couldn't succumb to the sweetness offered. "He's generous."

"He's given you more than the agreement?"

"My diamond wedding band, the tennis bracelet, the new car, Paul's clothes. But afterward I'm going to give everything but the clothes back to him."

"So his generosity is limited."

"He's kind to Paul," Susan hastily added.

"He didn't marry Paul."

"No, but he only married me for Gramp's sake."

Megan frowned. "He seems interested in you."

"He's a good actor. He pretends he's in love with me for Gramp's sake." He'd done such a good job of pretending, sometimes she forgot he was faking it.

Megan put her arms around her sister. "I'm sorry. I don't know what to say."

"Just don't agree to change schools, giving up your scholarship money. We can't afford that." Susan squeezed her tightly before standing and wiping her cheeks. "We'll be fine. At the end of this, we're going to be a lot better off, and we'll find a great place to live."

"But Rosa and Pedro will be here. Will you be able to find someone else to take care of Paul?"

"Of course. If nothing else, I can leave him with Kate's nanny. The biggest problem will be his missing Manuel and...and Zach."

And Paul wouldn't be the only one.

* * *

Zach tried to find some time alone with Susan that evening, but she kept Megan beside her. Or Paul. Or his grandfather. Or even Hester. Anyone but him.

He waited the standard half hour after she'd gone upstairs, but he ran up the stairs like a racer when the half hour was up.

Opening the door to the master bedroom, he stared into the half-lit room at the still form in the big bed.

Moving closer, he whispered, "Susan, are you awake?"

Her body jerked only slightly. If he hadn't been close, staring intently, he would've missed it. "I want to talk to you. I know you aren't asleep."

She still didn't move—until he sat down on the edge of the bed. Then she scurried to the other side and glared at him over her shoulder.

"You woke me up!"

"We both know that isn't true," he said calmly, offering a smile that didn't seem to please her.

She gave up the pretense. Sliding to a sitting position against the bed, she tugged the cover breast-high, leaving her shoulders, covered in a white T-shirt, exposed.

That damn white T-shirt, Zach thought.

"Is that what you always wear to bed?" he asked, forgetting his purpose for the visit.

"Yes, but why do you ask?"

He couldn't confess how many times that T-shirt had appeared in his dreams, how often he'd wanted to touch it and what was beneath. "Just curious. Most women prefer silk."

"I'm not most women," she snapped, and looked away.

"Did you think I was criticizing?" he asked with a laugh. "Honey, I've had fantasies about your T-shirt."

Her eyes widened in alarm and she shrank against the bed.

"Hey, I've kept my promise. You're not frightened, are you?" The thought cut him to the quick.

"No, of course not," she hurriedly said. "I just... Why did you want to talk to me?"

"I wanted to see if you were all right about Megan being here. And to tell you that I tried to keep Gramp from talking her into changing schools." She said nothing, so he risked adding, "Though I think it's a good idea. After all, I'm a KU alum."

"No."

She was staring straight ahead, not moving.

"Why?"

She turned to stare at him. "Zach, Megan changing schools won't affect Gramp's health. I've done everything you asked, but I can't do this. Leave Megan alone."

"Okay." He switched gears. "I need to talk to you about Paul."

"What's wrong? Did he do something wrong? Is he hurt? Do I need—"

"Hey, calm down," Zach said, raising one hand against her frantic questions. "Susan, Paul is family. We're not going to throw him out even if he *does* do something wrong. Gramp and I already love him. And Hester would beat anyone who laid a hand on him."

She rubbed her hands along her arms and ducked her head, hoping, he suspected, to hide the tears that filled her eyes. "I know," she whispered. "What— what did you want to say?"

"Paul and Manuel did some chores today, and they did a damn fine job." He took a deep breath, knowing he was about to cause an eruption. "I paid them."

"What? You paid them? For doing chores? That's ridiculous!"

"No, it's not. On the ranch, everyone is paid for their work. And the boys worked hard."

"But—I can't—no! Absolutely not!" She crossed her arms over her chest.

He sighed, his gaze lingering there. "Honey, it's a learning experience. The boys need practice handling money. I don't think Paul will be wasteful, but he needs to understand the relationship between sweat and hard work and money."

She bowed her head and covered her face with her hands. "You're changing everything, Zach. Everything!"

And he wanted to change even more.

Chapter Eleven

Megan returned to the University of Nebraska the next morning, driven by Zach's oldest cowboy, the one he hoped would be least affected by her youthful beauty.

In spite of Susan's resistance, Zach promised to send someone for Megan whenever she wanted to visit, and assured her he himself would come fetch her for Thanksgiving vacation.

He also gave her money. In a whispered exchange, he explained that he wanted her to have an emergency fund in case something went wrong. And he ordered her to call if she needed anything.

"But Gramp already gave me money," she whispered in return. "Really, I shouldn't take any."

He closed his hand around hers. "It's so we won't worry. You wouldn't want Gramp to have a setback, worrying about you, would you?" He was beginning to feel guilty using his grandfather's illness the way he was. But the women in his life were so caring, it worked like a charm.

"No, of course not," Megan said, her eyes widening in alarm.

"Good."

She reminded him so much of Susan, but she wasn't Susan. Megan's sister was special. And the one woman in the world who drove him crazy. Last night, he'd gathered her in his arms to comfort her. But he'd kept his promise. He hadn't made love to her. He hadn't even kissed her, because he knew he'd lose control if he did.

And that damned cold shower hadn't helped much.

After Megan was sent on her way, Paul touched Zach's arm.

"Yeah, buddy?"

"Do you have any more work for us today?" He ducked his head, then looked up at Zach. "I don't mean for money. Me and Manuel liked working."

"Did you talk to your sister?"

Paul smiled even more. "She said I could keep the money as long as I promised to save some of it." He shrugged his shoulders. "I'm going to save *all* of it. Then when Susan is sad and crying 'cause she can't pay the bills, I'll be able to help."

Zach couldn't stop himself. He swung the little boy into his arms for a bear hug. "You are one special guy, Paul. But I'll tell you what. I'll take care of Susan and her bills. You save your money for your own woman one day."

"Yuck! I don't want a girl!"

"Then maybe on Saturday we can go to town and spend part of it. I heard there's a new Disney movie showing at the theater."

"Go to a movie? Really? Wow, that'd be neat! And Manuel could come?"

"Of course. Hester might want to go with you, too, and include Josefina."

"Josie? She's a girl!"

"Yeah," Zach agreed with a grin.

Zach got back to the house early that afternoon and hit the shower. While dressing, he thought about taking Susan to town on Saturday while the boys were in the movies and buying her some boots.

After all, she was a rancher's wife.

That thought put a big grin on his face. He stepped over to her closet, wanting to be sure she didn't already have a pair.

The two closets in the master suite were huge. A waste of space in Susan's case. Zach was shocked to discover the cavernous emptiness. Six hangers were in use, and there were two pairs of shoes.

He frowned as he ran through his memories of Susan's wardrobe. She had worn that light blue knit several times already, and he'd only known her a week and a half. That navy suit he'd seen a couple of times, too. Her clothes were of good quality, but there weren't a lot of them.

"What are you doing?" she demanded from behind him.

He spun around. "You're home early!"

"A good thing. I didn't expect you to paw through my belongings." Her righteous anger brought bright color to her cheeks.

"I didn't mean to intrude, honey. I was thinking that you needed cowboy boots, so I wanted to check and see if you already had some."

She reached past him and shut the door to her closet. "No, I don't need any."

"Of course you do. You're a rancher's wife," he said, repeating the justification he'd already used to himself.

He would've turned into a Popsicle if her look had the power to transmit its chill.

"No."

"Susan, I want to teach you to ride. It isn't safe to ride without the proper equipment." And he wanted to see her in jeans. That was next on his list.

"I don't have time to ride."

Why was she so uptight today? Last night, as she'd cried in his arms, he'd felt closer to her than ever. "Did you have a bad day?"

"No."

"Something's the matter," he protested in frustration. "Last night—"

"I don't want to talk about last night. I—I was weak. It won't happen again."

She turned away, but he couldn't let her go. Catching her arm, he pulled her back to face him. "Whatever has put a burr under your saddle needs to be talked out, honey. If you go downstairs angry, everyone is going to be upset.''

''I won't let it show. After all,'' she snapped, ''I've proved what a good actress I am. Almost as good as you.''

''Okay,'' he said in even tones, as if everything were normal. ''Then plan on a shopping trip Saturday. You can show me how good an actress you are then.''

''I'm not going shopping with you.''

''You have to have more clothes than what's in that closet, Susan. You barely have enough for a week. Everyone has more than—''

''But I'm not everyone. I'm Susan Greenwood. You'll just have to deal with that, Zach, because I'm not going to allow you to buy my soul!'' Her voice had risen as she protested until she was almost shouting when she finished.

He didn't know what was going on. But he knew what to do. Without another word, he wrapped his arms around her and held her against him.

She struggled, protesting.

But he held on, not putting any moves on her, just holding her. Comforting her.

Finally, she realized she wasn't going to get away. Her body slumped against his and the room grew still.

When her breathing had returned to normal, he whispered, ''I know things have changed quickly, honey, but it's all for a good cause. Gramp is thriving, happier than I've ever seen him. You've given an old man a lot of happiness in the past few days.''

He stopped, but she said nothing. Her face was

buried against his neck and he inhaled her scent, loving the sweet, spicy perfume she always wore.

"You've also made me happy. I didn't believe a woman like you existed. You're the best mother I've ever seen, honey, and they're not even your children."

She pushed against him, and he reluctantly let her out of his embrace. Turning away from him and wiping her hands across her cheeks, Susan mumbled, "Thank you, Zach. But, please, don't buy me anything else. I can't...it's too overwhelming. I feel like I'm losing myself."

So she was rejecting the only thing he had to give her, since she didn't want him. Darkness filled him. If he lost her, life wouldn't be worth living.

She sniffed, and his eyes narrowed. Maybe there was still hope. Maybe she just needed time to adjust. He had until next May. Was he pushing too hard?

Probably. He'd never been known for his patience. After taking a deep breath to restore his optimism, he moved to her side and cupped one wet cheek in his hand. "Okay, sunshine, I won't force my riches on you. But remember, I'm in your debt, not the other way around. Okay?"

She gave him a wavery smile, nodding slightly, and he had to fight hard to keep from taking her lips with his.

Patience.

That was the ticket.

"You're being too patient!" Gramp roared.

"Look, Gramp, I know you're feeling better, but

you're not supposed to get upset."

"Lord have mercy, the little girl ignored you at dinner."

Zach sighed. "Gramp, she had a hard day. Give her some time. There have been a lot of changes in her life, not of her making, the past few days."

"Paul's had a lot of changes, too. He's okay."

"Paul's a little boy. As long as Susan is with him and his tummy is full, he's not going to complain."

Pete grinned. "Yeah. He's a fine boy, isn't he?"

"The best. Did I tell you what he's saving his money for?" He repeated his conversation with Paul, knowing it would touch his grandfather's heart.

"Damn fine boy!"

"Yeah."

"Heard from Megan since she went back to school?" Pete asked eagerly.

"She just left yesterday," Zach reminded him drily.

"I think we need to get her a car, a good one, so she can come home whenever she wants. I don't like her being that far away without transportation."

Zach smiled. He was beginning to see where he got his impatience from. And he was looking at his grandfather's suggestions from Susan's point of view.

"No. We can't interfere with the way Susan wants to raise her family."

"Damn it, we're family, too!"

Zach shook his head. "Not yet. If Susan and I— *when* Susan and I come to terms with what's happened, then we'll talk about making some changes. But I think we'll have to let Susan initiate them. We've acted like steamrollers, Gramp.''

Pete grumbled. "She unhappy?''

Zach's throat tightened. "Yeah. It's all been a little overwhelming for her.''

Pete stared at him, his eyes narrowing in speculation that made Zach uneasy. His grandfather was a master manipulator.

"How long?''

"Gramp, I don't know. Maybe a month or two.''

"A month? You got to get started on those babies sooner than that!''

For the first time in ages, Zach felt anger toward his grandfather. He'd been a rebellious teen, but in recent years, mindful of his grandfather's health, he'd seldom crossed the old man.

He stood. "Gramp, whether we have babies or not, Susan's happiness is important to me. I won't force her into anything…and you'd better not, either.'' He stomped from the room, hoping he had put a stop to the old man's push for a next generation.

Even if he agreed with him.

Because making babies with Susan was something he dreamed about every night.

Susan was reluctant to leave work.

It had become her refuge.

She went into the serving area of the diner and got herself a cup of coffee. Fortunately, Brenda wasn't busy, because Susan wasn't sure she could refill coffee cups today. It reminded her too much of the day she had met Zach.

"Susan! You're still here," Maggie called as she stepped into the diner.

"Yeah. What are you doing here so late?"

"Just wrapping up the end-of-the-month statement. We're getting better all the time," Maggie told her with a smile. The profits had been small after all the salaries were paid, but Kate's expertise was becoming known. The catering business was taking over the diner's return.

"Great."

Maggie's eyes narrowed. Then she said, "Mind if I join you in a cup? Do you have time?"

"Yes." She poured a cup for Maggie and automatically turned to the family booth. She almost asked Maggie if they could sit somewhere else, but she knew she couldn't. Maggie would know at once something was wrong.

"How are Ginny and James?" she asked as they sat down. Anything to keep from talking about her situation.

"Fine. Ginny is as bossy as ever," Maggie said with a smile. "I swear she was a drill sergeant in another life."

Susan chuckled. "I'm sure she'll outgrow it."

"Hopefully. How are you?"

"Me?" Susan asked, hoping she sounded cheerful. "Just fine."

"Are you? You seem a little edgy to me."

"Oh, I'm worried about the brochure. I finished it and Kate said she'd let me know."

"Didn't she call you? She brought it by the house this morning. We both love it. She was so excited, she was taking it to the printer at once."

"Oh, great! I wanted it to be…special. To say thank you for all you two have done for me."

Maggie gave her a disgusted look. "You are so stubborn! We're *family*. We do things for one another. I might never have gotten Josh to notice me without your makeover. I still say you could set up a business with that skill and get rich at it."

Susan gave a genuine smile this time. "Not hardly. I had terrific material to work with. And we both know Josh was already in love with you."

"And is Zach already in love with you?"

Maggie had slipped that question in when Susan thought she was safe. She lost her breath and her eyes teared. "No! No, he's not! It's all a game. I told you."

Maggie reached across the table to take Susan's hand. "Take a deep breath. I didn't mean to upset you."

"It's just…so many things have changed. Zach is being very nice, but it's for his grandfather's sake." And she worked hard to remember that when he touched her, held her. She tried so hard, but she feared she was losing the battle. One of these days, she'd attack him and then never be able to face him again.

"Is this private or can I join in?" Kate asked, a cup of coffee in her hand.

"J-join us," Susan said, hoping they could talk about business now, or about her sisters' babies, or the weather, or anything but Zach Lowery.

After a quick exchange of glances with Maggie, Kate said, "Susan, the brochure was brilliant! The printer was practically drooling over your work. He wanted to know if you'd take on any other clients."

Whatever she'd been expecting, it wasn't an offer for more business. "I don't think... I mean, I'm working for our company."

"I know, but now that the brochure is done, how much work is there? I think you'd have time to do the work, and you could do it here." Kate smiled ruefully. "At least, I hope that's what you want, 'cause I told him yes."

It was Maggie who scolded her. "Kate, that's Susan's decision!"

"I know, I know. But I told him you were expensive. We agreed that you wouldn't do a brochure for less than five thousand."

Susan choked. "That much? But—"

"And a bargain at that price," Kate announced, as if no one would have the nerve to argue with her.

Her two sisters watched her expectantly. Susan reached out a hand to each of them. "Thanks. That would be great."

Kate gave a relieved sigh. "I'm glad. I didn't want to run over you, the way Zach has."

Susan stiffened. "He's only doing it for his grandfather's sake."

"He hasn't done anything you don't like, has he?" Maggie asked, watching her closely.

Susan could feel her cheeks heating up. She didn't want to think about the kisses, the hugs, the comfort he'd given her. She shouldn't like it…but she did.

"No, of course not. And he's been wonderfully kind to Paul and Megan."

"Megan? Is Megan at the ranch?" Kate demanded.

"No, not now. But I left a message for her with the ranch phone number in case of an emergency. She found out I was married and was waiting for me Monday."

"Is she okay with everything?"

"Yes, but…the Lowery men are overpowering. Gramp immediately wanted her to transfer to KU so she'd be closer to the ranch."

"How did Megan feel about it?"

"Oh, she was ready. She said she was too lonesome in Nebraska."

"Susie, let Maggie and me pay her tuition wherever she wants to go. You know I don't need the money from the diner. Maggie doesn't, either, both because of Josh and her own successful business. Pop would be so proud if he thought the diner was providing for you."

"Kate's right," Maggie added. "And we could start a fund for Paul, so he'd have a choice, too."

Tears streamed down Susan's cheeks. She never used to cry. At least not in front of people. Now she seemed a veritable fountain. "You're so generous. But really, it's not necessary."

"We know. But we still want to do it," Maggie said softly.

Susan squeezed their hands. "I—I think that would be great," she finally agreed.

Her sisters appeared stunned by her capitulation. "Terrific!" Kate finally responded. "We'll set up a trust fund for each of them. When will Megan transfer? Can we—"

Susan held up a hand. "Wait! There's a condition."

She gathered her thoughts, then said, "I want you not to tell Megan until after May."

"Why?" Kate demanded.

"Because once we leave the ranch, it might affect her decision. I've explained that the marriage isn't permanent, but Zach and his grandfather are so...so convincing, that I'm not sure she's accepted my explanation." She drew in a large gulp of air. "Fairy tales are so believable."

"Of course we'll wait," Maggie agreed, ignoring Kate's sharp look. "But we'll still pay for room and board the second semester. We'll just give the money to you."

"No, I have enough for—"

"Don't go back on your word," Kate chided. "Buy something for yourself. Or put it in savings. This one's on Pop."

Susan blinked back her tears. She'd never known her father, but her sisters were the most wonderful people in the world. "Thank you so much."

"No thanks necessary. Now, we'd all better get home to our menfolk," Kate said, looking at her watch. "Things are looking up for the O'Connor girls, but we'd best take care of business, as Pop used to say."

They all got up, and Susan hurried to her office to get her purse. Then she waved goodbye to her sisters and headed for the ranch. She didn't mind going home now. Her prospects were improving. She was going to be able to pay her own way.

Maggie and Kate stood at the door of the diner, watching as Susan drove away.

"Is she as miserable as I think she is?" Kate asked.

"Absolutely."

"Will everything work out all right?" Kate asked, seeking reassurance.

Maggie sighed. "I don't know. But she's beginning to open up, to let us in. I think loving Zach has made a difference."

"Men! They always get the credit," Kate protested with a grin.

"Yeah. I only hope Zach realizes how fortunate he is," Maggie said, her gaze filled with worry.

"If he doesn't, we'll send Josh and Will out to beat him up."

Maggie chuckled. "They'd probably end up commiserating with him. They were just as miserable until we settled everything."

"True. I think Susan will work things out by herself. After all, she's an O'Connor, whether she claims the name or not. The Lucky Charm is working for her, as it did for us."

"Yes," Maggie agreed. "Pop would be so proud."

Chapter Twelve

Zach was encouraged Wednesday night. Susan came home in a good mood, even sparing him a smile or two at dinner.

He'd been right. Patience was the key. Now if he could just convince his body of that theory. Because when winter came, cold showers weren't going to be a lot of fun.

"Rosa and I took the boys and Josie to school to register today," he mentioned to Susan.

"You did? Paul? Did everything go okay?"

"Sure. I met my new teacher. She liked Zach a lot." Paul helped himself to more mashed potatoes.

Susan turned to stare at Zach. "I'm sure she did," she said coolly.

Zach hastily clarified Paul's comment. "She's an old friend. A *married* old friend. We went to school together."

"How nice," Susan said, turning her attention to her meal.

"Manny and I are in the same class," Paul added.

"I'm glad," Susan said, "but I'd better not get a report that you're not paying attention and doing your work." Her brother nodded, unconcerned with her strictures. "What time will you leave for school each morning? I can drop the two of you off when I leave."

"Zach said he could take us in his truck," Paul said, watching his sister for her reaction.

Zach hurriedly intervened. "It would be better if your sister took you, buddy. I might have some things to do here."

Susan gave him a searching look but said nothing.

"How's your work going, Susan?" Pete suddenly asked.

"Very well."

"You one of those career women?"

Zach almost groaned aloud. "Uh, Gramp—"

"I'm not sure what you mean, Gramp. I like my work."

Pete, who was now eating at the dinner table instead of in bed, leaned forward. "I mean, when you have babies, you're not going to insist on working, are you?"

"Gramp," Zach said, jumping in, "Susan doesn't need to worry about that right now."

Again Susan sent him a sharp look, as if she suspected him of something. Hell, he was trying to keep the pressure off of her. A lot of appreciation he was getting for it.

"Just thinking ahead, boy," Pete protested.

"Well, you'd better eat your dinner. There's a great movie starting in a few minutes. I thought we all might watch it together."

That got everyone's attention, and Zach breathed a sigh of relief. He was going to have another talk with Gramp. He couldn't survive too many more dinners with Gramp playing a heavy-handed Cupid.

In the den, as they all settled down to watch the movie, Gramp maneuvered Zach and Susan onto the couch, encouraging Paul to sit beside his sister while pushing her closer to Zach.

Okay, so Zach was going to be patient, but he couldn't resist wrapping his arm around Susan a few minutes after the movie started. She rested against him, laying her head on his shoulder, her warmth enveloping him, and he scarcely saw any of the movie.

Zach was working in the far corral, putting a young filly through her paces, when Hester came puffing to the fence railing.

"Zach?" she called.

He led the horse over to the railing. "Hi, Hester. Is anything wrong?"

"No. Just a message from Susan. She asked you to meet her at the Plaza Hotel at five o'clock."

Zach frowned. "Did she say why?"

"Nope. Said she had some errands to run and

would meet you there.'' Hester turned to go back to the house.

Zach asked one more time, "You're sure it was Susan? And she said the Plaza at five o'clock.''

"Yep. I figured you'd need all the time you could to get cleaned up and make it on time.'' Then she walked away.

Zach stared at his dusty jeans, rubbed the stubble on his chin and realized Hester was right. He'd have to hurry. And he guessed it didn't really matter why Susan had sent the message. He released the filly into a nearby pasture and sprinted for the house.

Half an hour later, he jumped into his truck, the dust and stubble gone. He was still dressed in jeans, but he brought a suit with him in a hanging bag, just in case Susan had something dressy in mind.

"Good evening, Mr. Lowery,'' the man behind the check-in desk greeted him. "Here's your key. Everything's arranged.''

Zach raised his eyebrows. "Okay, thank you. Is Mrs. Lowery here?''

"Not yet, sir.''

Zach discovered they were booked into the honeymoon suite again. Had Susan changed her mind? Was she interested in more than she'd originally said?

Those thoughts had him jabbing at the button on the elevator several times, impatient. Then he drew a deep breath. He'd promised patience. He'd let Susan make the first move.

Then he'd be able to satisfy his frustrations.

Oh mercy...

He slid the key into the door and carried his hanging bag through to the master bedroom closet. On the way back into the other room, he saluted the large bed.

No couch tonight.

He paced the length of the living room several times before he noticed the tray on the table. Another bottle of champagne waited in a bucket of ice.

Susan was going all out, he decided with a smile. Until he remembered her inexperience with the bubbly. Eyes narrowing, he approached the table.

Beside the bucket with the champagne was a note. Frowning, Zach picked it up.

Patience isn't working. Enjoy.

Zach closed his eyes with a groan. Gramp.

The door opened to admit Susan.

"Zach? What's going on? Why was I supposed to meet you here?" She came closer, her gaze falling on the champagne. She came to a halt, her widened stare returning to Zach. "What's going on?"

He crumpled the note behind his back. "Uh, Gramp wanted us to have some time alone."

Before Susan could respond, someone knocked on the door.

Zach crossed the room and pulled it open to find an older man in a dark suit, holding several boxes. "Good evening, Zach. I'm James Pruitt, the manager here. Your grandfather sent some gifts for you and Mrs. Lowery."

Zach had no choice but to take the boxes. He set them down on the end of the sofa. James Pruitt held out an envelope. When Zach took it, the manager bowed and left.

In the envelope were tickets to a performance at Starlight Theater, the outdoor theater that operated all summer, as well as a note indicating dinner would be at seven o'clock.

"Damn," Zach muttered. Gramp was determined to push Susan into a real marriage.

"It's all right. Your grandfather doesn't understand. We can—"

"These are tickets to the Starlight. Dinner for two in the restaurant downstairs. And, just at a guess, I think he probably bought us clothes."

To his surprise, Susan opened the two boxes. One held a suit for him, ordered from his favorite clothing store. Zach didn't want to think what Gramp had had to pay for such fast delivery.

In the other box was a blue dress, shimmery and feminine, that made Susan gasp. "Oh, it's beautiful."

"It'll look even better with you wearing it. Want to go to the theater?"

"I don't want to upset Gramp."

Oh, he was tempted. To have an evening, a night, with Susan, had been his hope when he'd arrived. But he couldn't take advantage of her.

"Honey," he began, then had to clear his throat. The thought of what he was denying himself was painful. "Honey, Gramp knows."

She stared at him, uncomprehending. Then, her voice huskier than ever, she said, "He knows? He knows we're not married?"

"We are married! We're just not—not really married."

She dropped the dress back into the box. "You told him?"

"No, he figured it out."

"That's a relief," she said, slowly sinking onto the couch. "That means— When did he tell you?"

"Monday, the day Megan came to the ranch."

As his answer sunk in, her anger rose. "That's four days ago! You let me continue to believe that we had to pretend to—pretend to be in love?" She advanced toward him. "How could you? How could you torment me even one day, Zach Lowery? You knew—"

"I knew that you were safe, taken care of, settled. I should have told you and upset you?" he asked, not sure what his response should be.

She backed away from him, looking for her purse. "We'll move out at once."

"You damn well won't! How dare you even think of such a thing. Just because Gramp knows doesn't mean your leaving wouldn't hurt him. And what about Paul? Are you going to separate him from his best friend, from Gramp, from *me?*"

Susan was hurting inside herself. She didn't want to leave Zach or the ranch. She didn't want to be on her own again. Loving Zach had made her weak, as she'd feared.

And now she couldn't stay.

"We have to go. I only agreed to stay until Gramp was recovered, and obviously he's recovered very well.'' She tried to move past Zach, but he blocked her way.

"You agreed to stay the entire school year. Until May. You promised. You promised Paul and me.''

She closed her eyes. If she didn't, he'd see how much she hated her decision. How much she wanted to stay.

"Let me go, Zach.''

"I *won't* let you go. I won't *ever* let you go.'' Then he pulled her against him, his lips taking hers.

How could she want him so much? How could she feel the wonder of his touch, when she knew she had to leave? Her mother had always given in to the physical. She wouldn't.

But Zach's hands stroked her body as his mouth continued its domination over hers. Her own hands crept up his chest to lock around his neck. He lifted his mouth, then returned it at another angle, asking more and more of her in response.

And, God help her, she responded.

Wrapped in his arms, she pressed closer and closer to him, wanting more, wanting to feel him inside her, to become one with this man whose very presence tortured her senses every day.

His hands left her hips to unbutton her jacket, then her blouse. She found the snaps on his Western shirt to be much more efficient. In one mighty pull, she exposed his broad, muscular chest. Her hands memorized it with loving caresses.

Suddenly, she realized they were moving, step by agonizing step, toward the bedroom. Susan knew what Zach intended. She also knew she could stop him at any time.

The decision was hers.

But for the first time in her life, she wanted a man, this man, with all her heart. Forever. Even if he never intended to love her.

She couldn't resist the temptation to give him her love, unstintingly. With a whimper as his lips left hers, she didn't fight their progress. In fact, she pulled his shirt out of his pants and shoved it down his arms. He helped by shrugging out of it, dropping it on the floor, then doing the same to her jacket and blouse.

The electric sparks that their touching ignited, the powerful surge of desire that filled her, numbed her to anything but Zach. The resistance she'd tried to maintain had melted away.

When they reached the bed, Zach stopped. Susan almost cried out as he caught her by her arms and held his tantalizing lips away from her.

"Honey, I'm not overpowering you, am I? Do you want this as much as I do?"

"Yes," she whispered. One word was all it took to make Zach dismiss any qualms, but Susan wasn't complaining. She'd saved herself for this moment, to become one with the one man in the world she loved.

Even if he didn't love her. At least he made her feel as if he did....

Zach was an artful lover, teasing her, encouraging her, touching her. She loved the feel of his hands on her body and returned the favor as much as she could. He was so strong, so loving.

When he was finally ready to enter her, Susan was so beside herself with need, with hunger, that she pleaded with him to take her.

He did.

And gasped her name. "Susan!"

The pain was minimal, the joy of communion immense. "Yes, please, Zach."

His lips took hers again and they mated, as lovers do, but Susan didn't think anyone could ever have experienced such incredible happiness.

Her first time.

He'd wanted to share a first with her the last time they'd been together in this suite, but he hadn't dared. Now he'd experienced the ultimate first with Susan.

And he only loved her more.

His woman, his wife, was loving, kind, selfless and incredibly sexy. He gathered her against him afterward, his lips kissing her brow. "You should've told me," he whispered.

She froze. "Why?"

"So I'd take better care of you, Susan. Are you all right?"

"Yes. Did I do something wrong?"

"Hell, no! If you were any better, I might not've survived."

She relaxed against him, and he noted her drooping eyelids.

"Go to sleep, honey. We'll talk later."

He held her until she slept, his gaze trained on her

beautiful face. Even as she dozed, he couldn't resist touching her, to reassure himself that she was his.

Several hours later, Susan awoke to find herself alone. Her heart constricted as she thought about what had happened. She and Zach had made love—or at least it was love on her part. Zach probably figured they'd had good sex.

"Good heavens!" she muttered as she realized she had taken no precautions to prevent pregnancy.

Just like her mother.

"No," she whispered. No, she wouldn't be like her mother. She was already different because she loved Zach. As she'd never loved anyone else on earth. And if their lovemaking made a child, she'd take care of it.

She'd never abandon or neglect it, as her mother had with her children.

Susan sagged against the pillow, relieved to discover that a lot of her father, Mike O'Connor, must be in her. He'd taken care of his two children.

But she also faced the fact that she had to leave the ranch, even if it did cause Gramp and Paul, and maybe even Zach, a lot of unhappiness. Because she couldn't go back to the ranch and not make love with Zach.

And she couldn't continue to share such intimacy with him without his caring.

And since he was planning on her leaving in May, he didn't care the way she did.

She shoved back the covers, planning to get

dressed, when the door opened. Immediately she yanked the cover to her chest.

"You're awake?" Zach said, a lazy, satisfied smile on his face. "Want some dinner?"

He was wrapped in a terry-cloth robe, looking even sexier than before. Susan's mouth watered. She couldn't believe she wanted him again, now. "No, thank you."

"Honey, it's after seven. Sorry I didn't wait dinner on you, but I was starved. Sure you don't want to eat something?"

She closed her eyes. "No, thank you. I'd better get dressed and—"

"You want to go to the theater?" he asked, his voice rising, as if he thought she was crazy.

What was wrong with the man? He was acting as if their making love was normal, everyday, expected. "No! I'm—I'm going to the ranch to start packing."

His eyes widened, then he closed the bedroom door behind him and came across to the bed. "What are you talking about?"

"I can't stay there any longer, Zach." She fought hard to hold back the tears her words brought.

"Why not?"

Anger rose in her. "You think I can pretend that we have a real marriage? That it's going to last? I signed that piece of paper. I'm moving out next May. I can't—"

He pulled her into his arms and kissed her, a long, deep kiss, a kiss that brought back the lovemaking they'd shared. She wasn't sure she was breathing when he took his mouth away.

"You're not leaving, Susan Lowery. Not now and not next May. Not ever. I'll burn that piece of paper. I'll eat it myself if I have to. But I'm not letting you leave." His frown was ferocious as he stared at her.

"Why?" Her quiet question seemed to take him by surprise, but she had to know the answer before her heart burst from hope.

"Because I love you," he whispered. "I never thought I'd love a woman, but you stormed into my life with your sweetness, your concern, your determination to keep your distance." He kissed her again. When he raised his head this time, he said, "I can't let you go, honey. I found you at the Lucky Charm Diner and you're my personal four-leaf clover. With you, I've found happiness."

"Oh, Zach, I love you, too," she cried. "But I thought you were planning to end the marriage. That it was just for Gramp."

He curled his body around her, touching her from her head to her toes. "It *was* just for Gramp...in the beginning. But I couldn't resist you, honey."

Her arms circled his neck. "Zach, it's been so hard."

"Tell me about it," he said before he gave her another soul-shattering kiss.

"I suppose we should go tell everyone we're married," Susan said dreamily, her lips traveling over his face.

"Mmm, later," Zach suggested.

She didn't argue.

Epilogue

Susan lay against the pillows, listening as Zach talked to the bellboy in the living room. She hoped he'd hurry. She was starving.

The door swung open. "Dinner is served, my lady," Zach said with a grin. "You know, I think the staff gets as much pleasure out of our anniversary as we do."

"I doubt that," she said dreamily. This was their second wedding anniversary, and like last year, they'd come back to the Plaza to celebrate.

He rolled the table near the bed, filled a plate for Susan and handed it to her after she piled pillows behind her.

"Comfy?"

"I'll be more comfy if you come back to bed."

He brought his own plate with him as he stretched out beside her. Then he set it down to rub her protruding stomach. "How's Junior doing?"

"I think he's dancing a jig. It's my Irish blood."

"I hope he doesn't have your Irish temper," Zach teased.

She smiled. He might need an Irish temper to hold his own in their ever-expanding family. Kate had had a little girl in April. Both Susan and Maggie were due in November. Josh said they were having a race, but Susan didn't care which one delivered first.

"*I* think Junior is practicing his calf-roping."

Susan groaned and shifted a little closer to her husband. "I know he is if Paul has anything to do with it. The boy sleeps with that rope you gave him."

"He's getting pretty good, too. Gramp says he's better than me at that age. He's already planning a rodeo career for Paul."

"We'll discuss that later," Susan said. "But I'm taking the rope away from him if he uses it on Josie anymore."

Zach leaned over and kissed her. "Don't worry. I had a talk with him and Manuel about how a cowboy treats women."

"They might as well learn from an expert," she said softly, snuggling against her husband.

"Well, thank you very much, my little bride. But I think this cowboy needs more practice. I don't want to forget how to please you." He set his plate aside and took her into his arms.

And just as it had been the past two times they made love in this hotel, their dinner was forgotten.

Another tradition for the two of them.

* * * * *

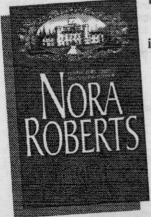
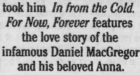

If you enjoyed what you just read,
then we've got an offer you can't resist!

Take 2 bestselling love stories FREE!

Plus get a FREE surprise gift!

Silhouette ROMANCE™

In March,
award-winning,
bestselling author
Diana Palmer joins
Silhouette Romance in
celebrating the one year
anniversary of its
successful promotion:

VIRGIN BRIDES

*Celebrate the joys of
first love with unforgettable
stories by our most beloved authors....*

**March 1999:
CALLAGHAN'S BRIDE
Diana Palmer**

Callaghan Hart exasperated temporary ranch cook
Tess Brady by refusing to admit that the attraction they
shared was more than just passion. Could Tess make
Callaghan see she was his truelove bride before her time
on the Hart ranch ran out?

Silhouette®

Available at your favorite retail outlet.

This March Silhouette is proud to present

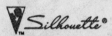

SENSATIONAL

MAGGIE SHAYNE
BARBARA BOSWELL
SUSAN MALLERY
MARIE FERRARELLA

This is a special collection of four complete novels for one low price, featuring a novel from each line: Silhouette Intimate Moments, Silhouette Desire, Silhouette Special Edition and Silhouette Romance.

Available at your favorite retail outlet.

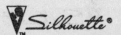

THESE BACHELOR DADS NEED A LITTLE TENDERNESS—AND A WHOLE LOT OF LOVING!

January 1999—A Rugged Ranchin' Dad
by Kia Cochrane (SR# 1343)

Tragedy had wedged Stone Tyler's family apart. Now this rugged rancher would do everything in his power to be the perfect daddy—and recapture his wife's heart—before time ran out....

April 1999 —Prince Charming's Return
by Myrna Mackenzie (SR# 1361)

Gray Alexander was back in town—and had just met the son he had never known he had. Now he wanted to make Cassie Pratt pay for her deception eleven years ago...even if the price was marriage!

And in **June 1999** don't miss Donna Clayton's touching story of Dylan Minster, a man who has been raising his daughter all alone....

Fall in love with our FABULOUS FATHERS!

And look for more FABULOUS FATHERS in the months to come. Only from

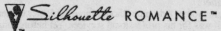

Available wherever Silhouette books are sold.

Look us up on-line at: http://www.romance.net   SRFFJ-J

Silhouette ROMANCE™

COMING NEXT MONTH

#1360 THE EXECUTIVE'S BABY—Robin Wells
Loving the Boss

When her former flame—and current boss—Nick Delaney asked
Rachel Sinclair to give him some badly needed daddy lessons, she
jumped at the chance to be part of this little family. But first she
needed to teach Nick that underneath her mommy skills was a
desirable woman....

#1361 PRINCE CHARMING'S RETURN—Myrna Mackenzie
Fabulous Fathers

Town prince Gray Alexander was back—and had just come face-to-
face with the son he never knew he'd had. Now he wanted to make
Cassie Pratt pay for her deception eleven years ago...even if the
price was marriage!

#1362 WES STRYKER'S WRANGLED WIFE—Sandra Steffen
Bachelor Gulch

Wes Stryker believed everyone had a destined lifelong partner—and
he'd just found his. Trouble was, Jayne Kincaid had vowed not to get
roped in by any man. So it was up to Wes to show this little lady that
she belonged in his ready-made family—and in his arms!

#1363 TRULY DADDY—Cara Colter

Rugged mountain man Garrett Boyd didn't know much about raising
a little girl. And the lost traveler who just landed on his doorstep
wasn't much help, either. Toni Carlton had never thought of herself
as mommy material, but with Garrett and his little girl by her side,
she started to think she could learn....

#1364 THE COWBOY COMES A COURTING—Christine Scott
He's My Hero

The last thing Skye Whitman intended to become was the wife
of a cowboy! And even though an accident had landed rodeo star
Tyler Bradshaw in her arms, she swore she wouldn't fall for him. Of
course Tyler was just as determined to make Skye do exactly that....

#1365 HIS PERFECT FAMILY—Patti Standard
Family Matters

When single mother Adrianne Rhodes hired carpenter Cutter
Matchett, it was for his professional services. Yet before long he was
rebuilding her home and her heart. But Cutter had a secret that, once
revealed, could bring them together—or tear them apart....